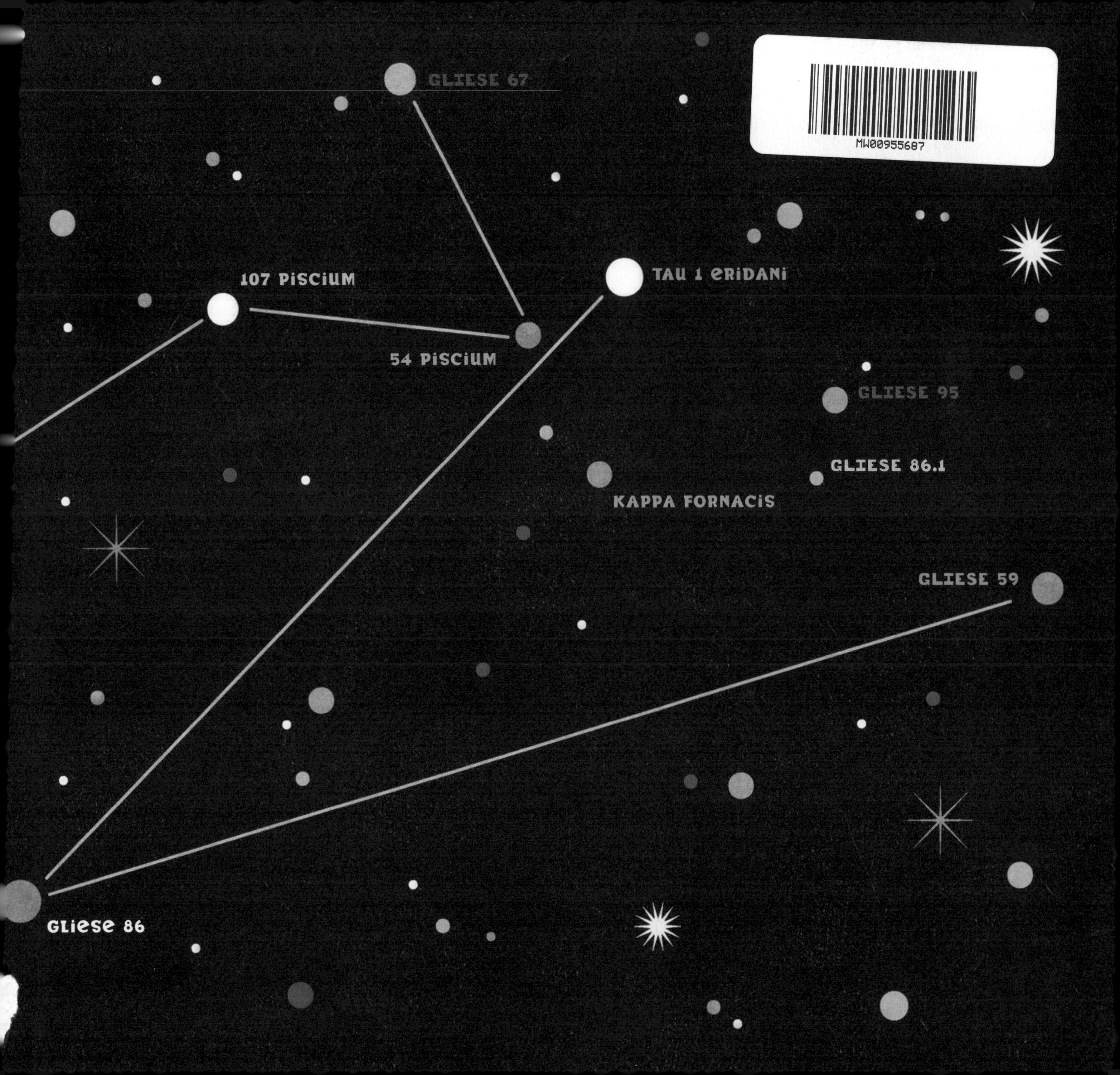
GLIESE 67
107 PISCIUM
TAU 1 ERIDANI
54 PISCIUM
GLIESE 95
GLIESE 86.1
KAPPA FORNACIS
GLIESE 59
GLIESE 86

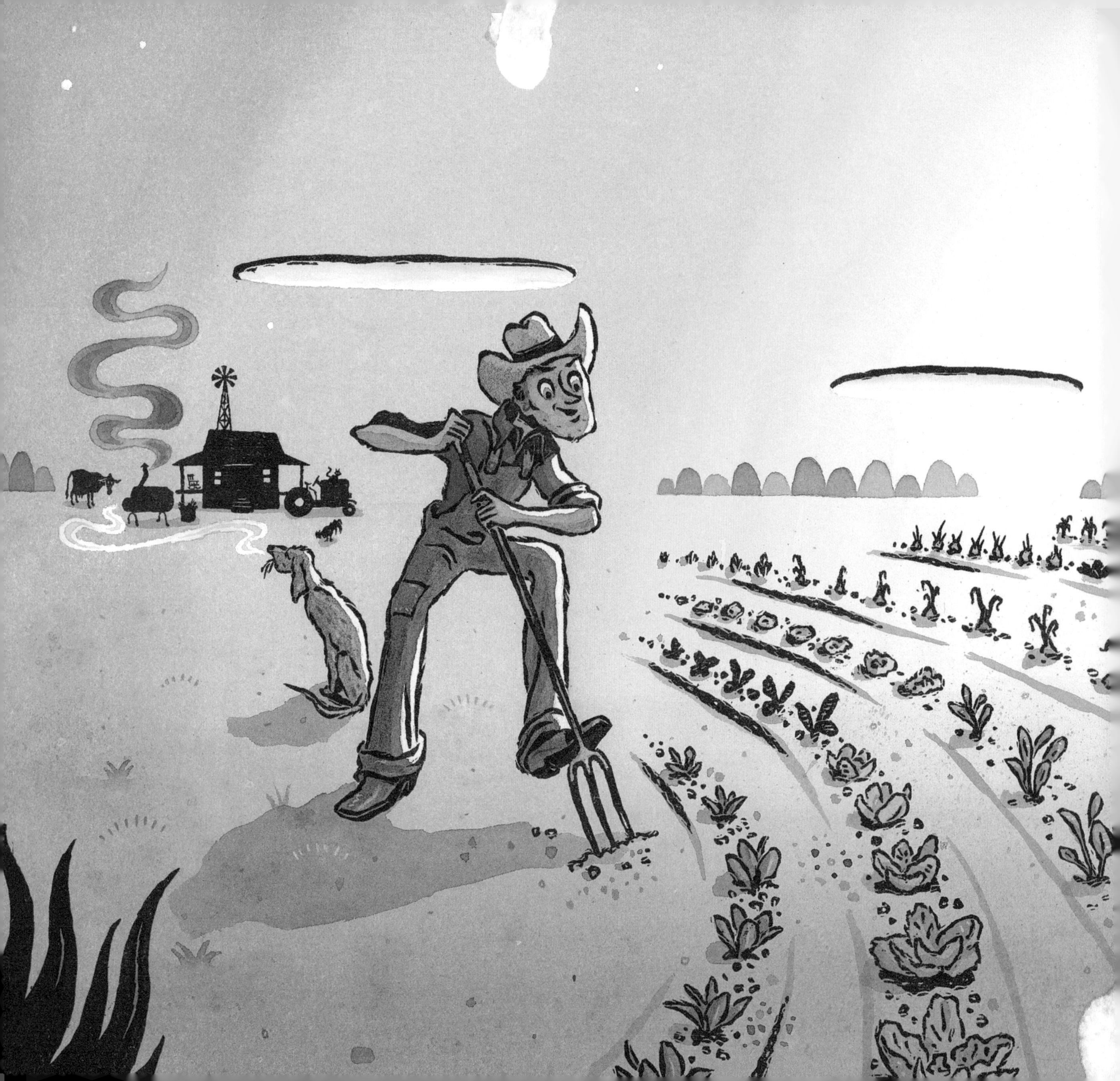

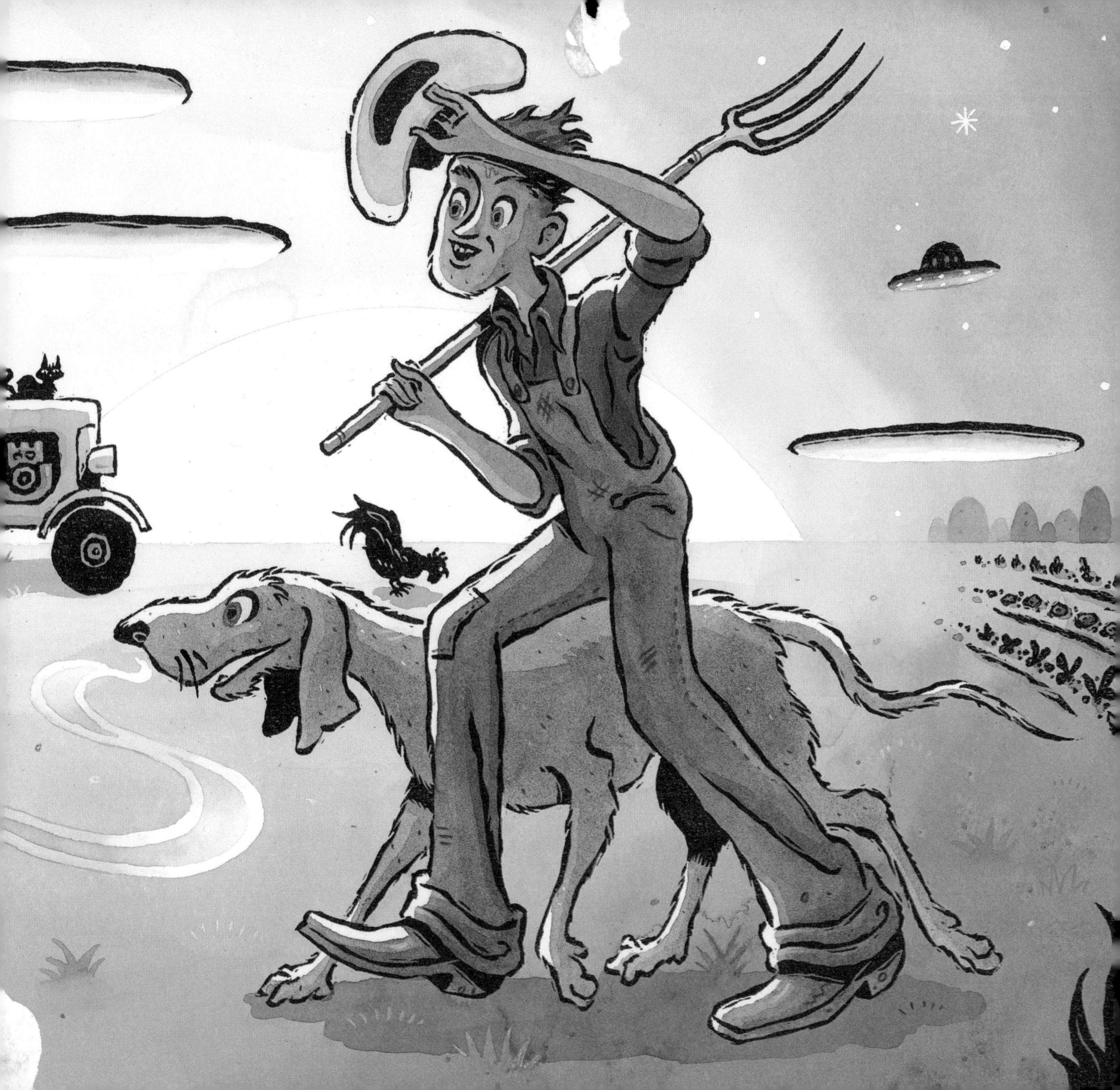

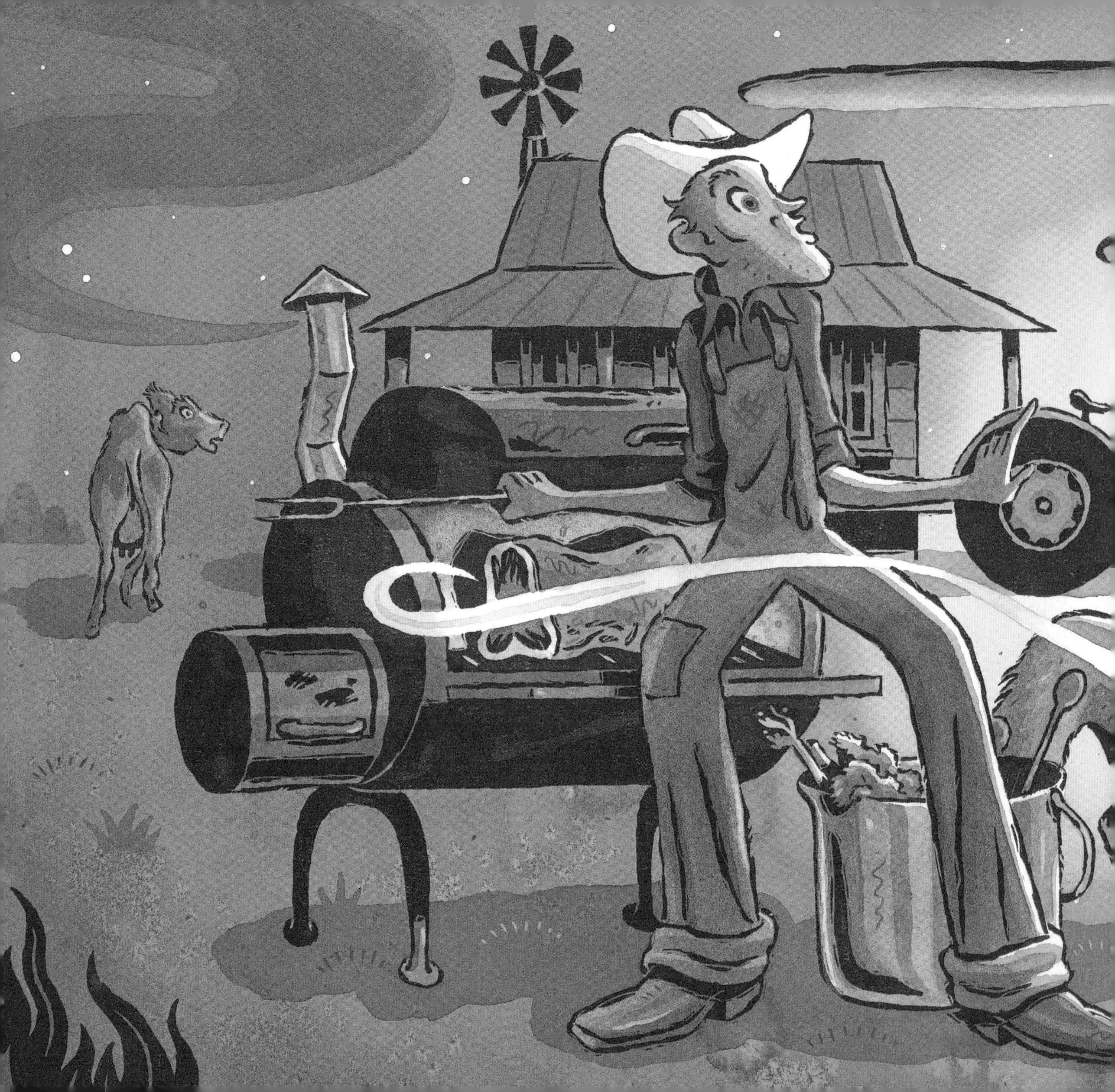

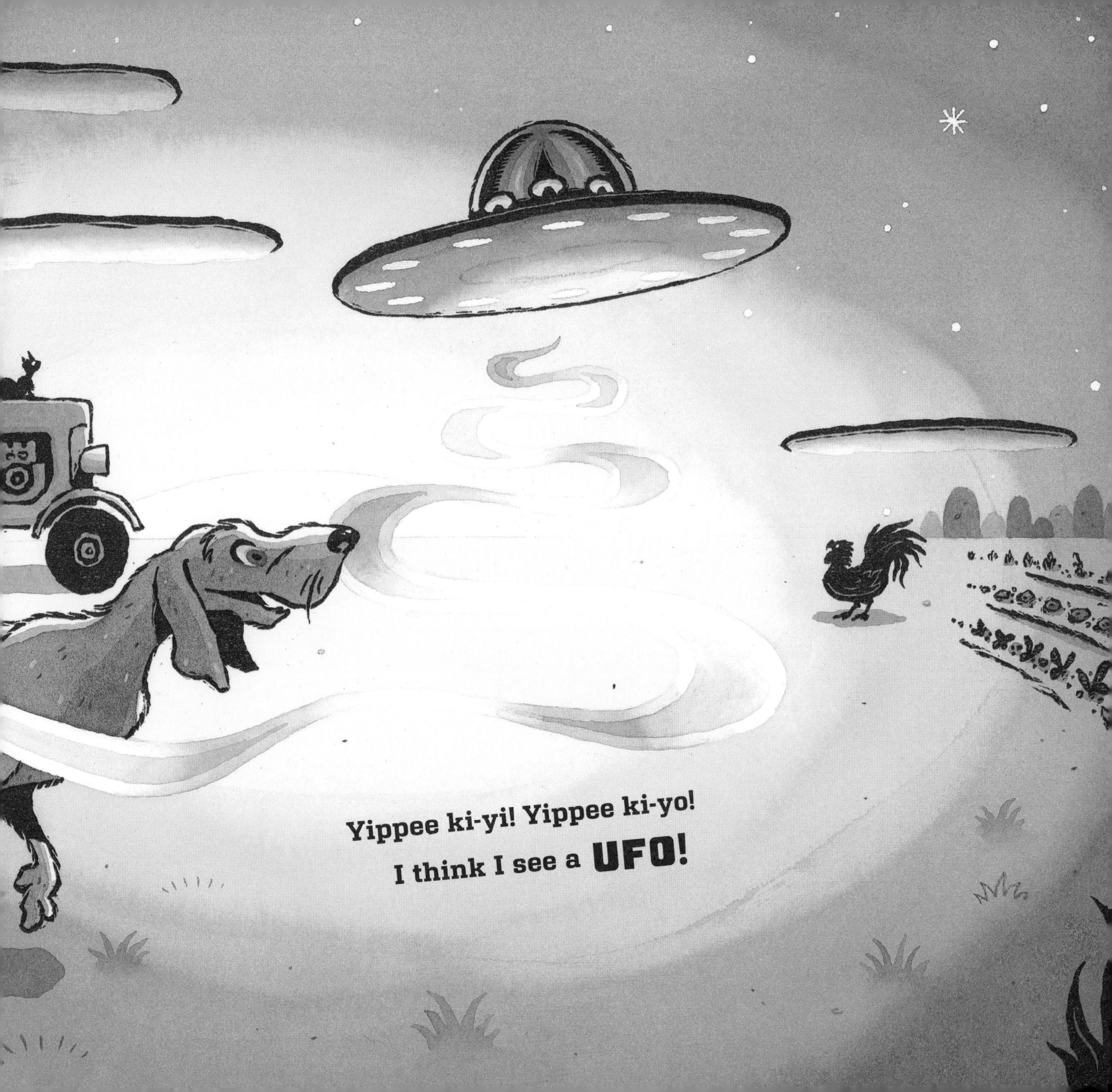

Yippee ki-yi! Yippee ki-yo!

I think I see a **UFO**!

Some colored lights from outer space
Are lightin' up the whole dang place!

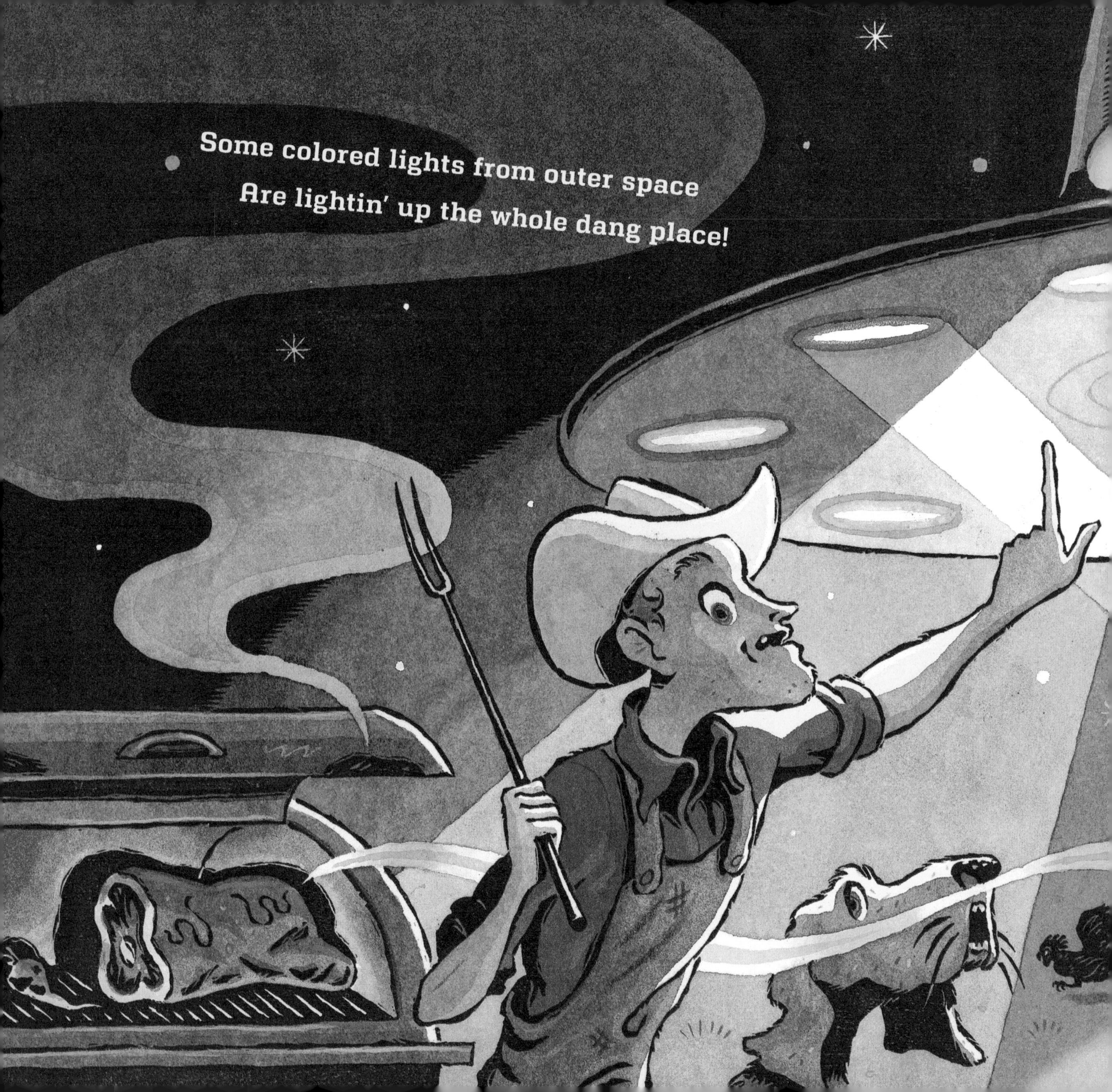

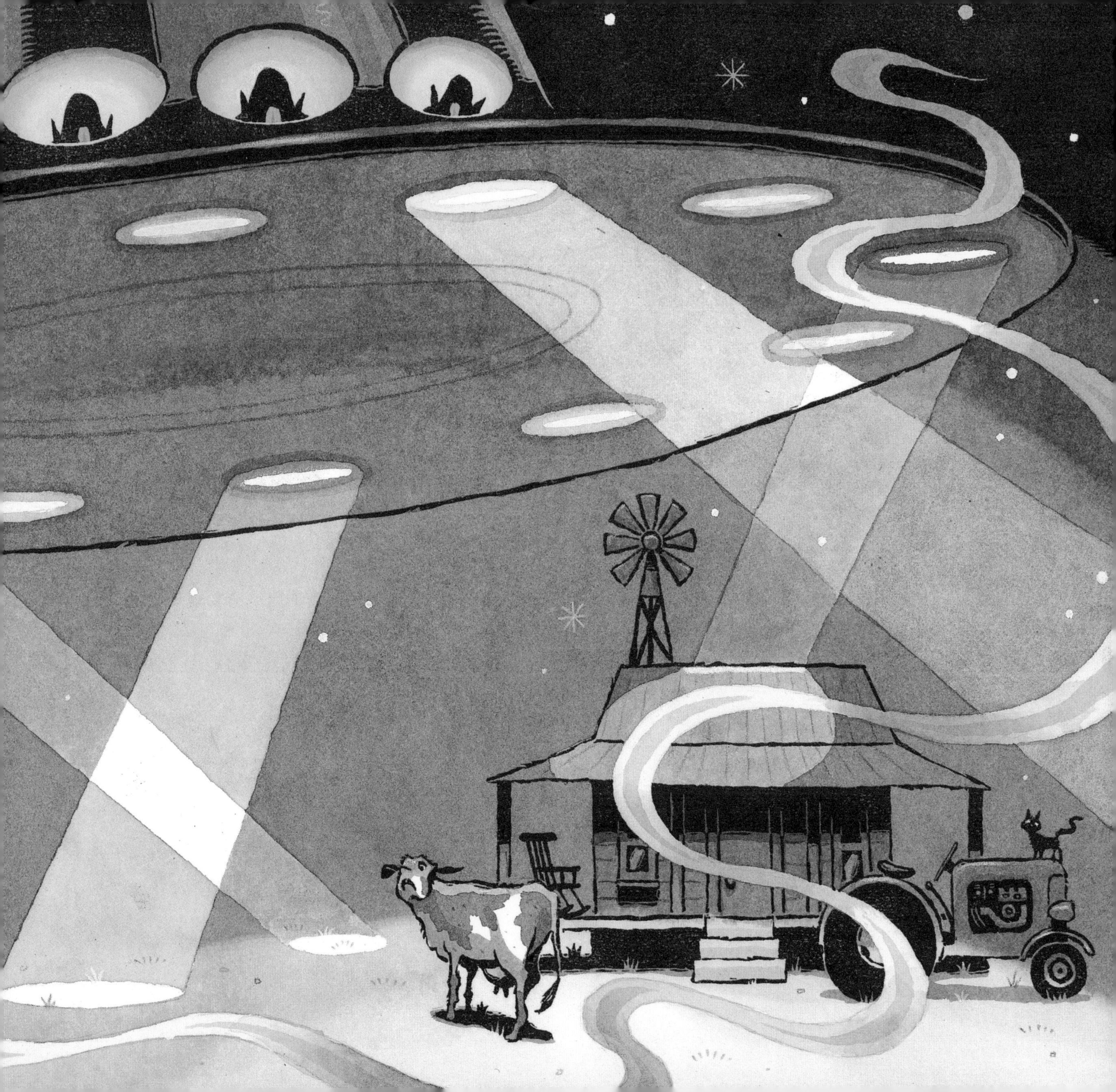

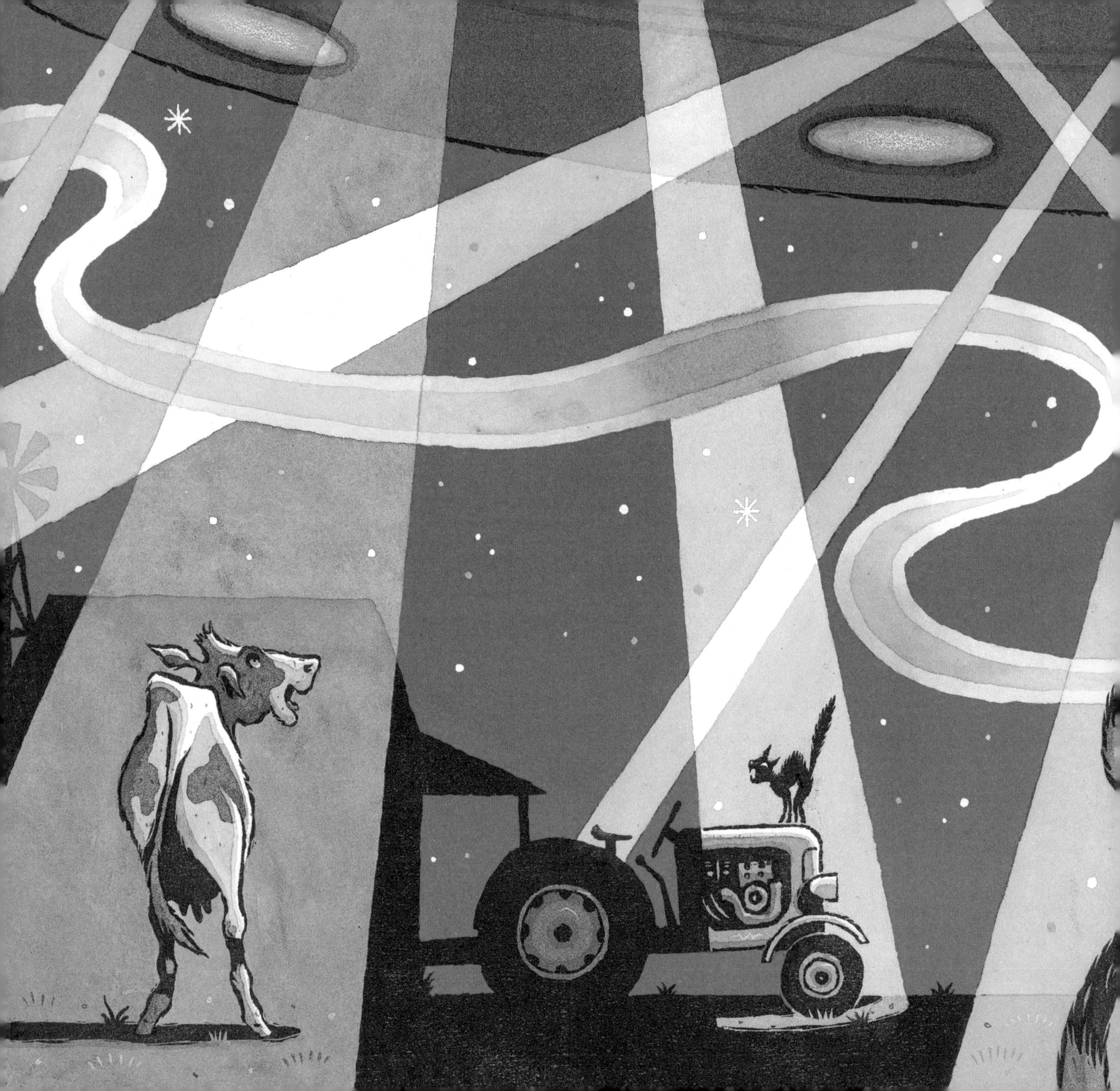

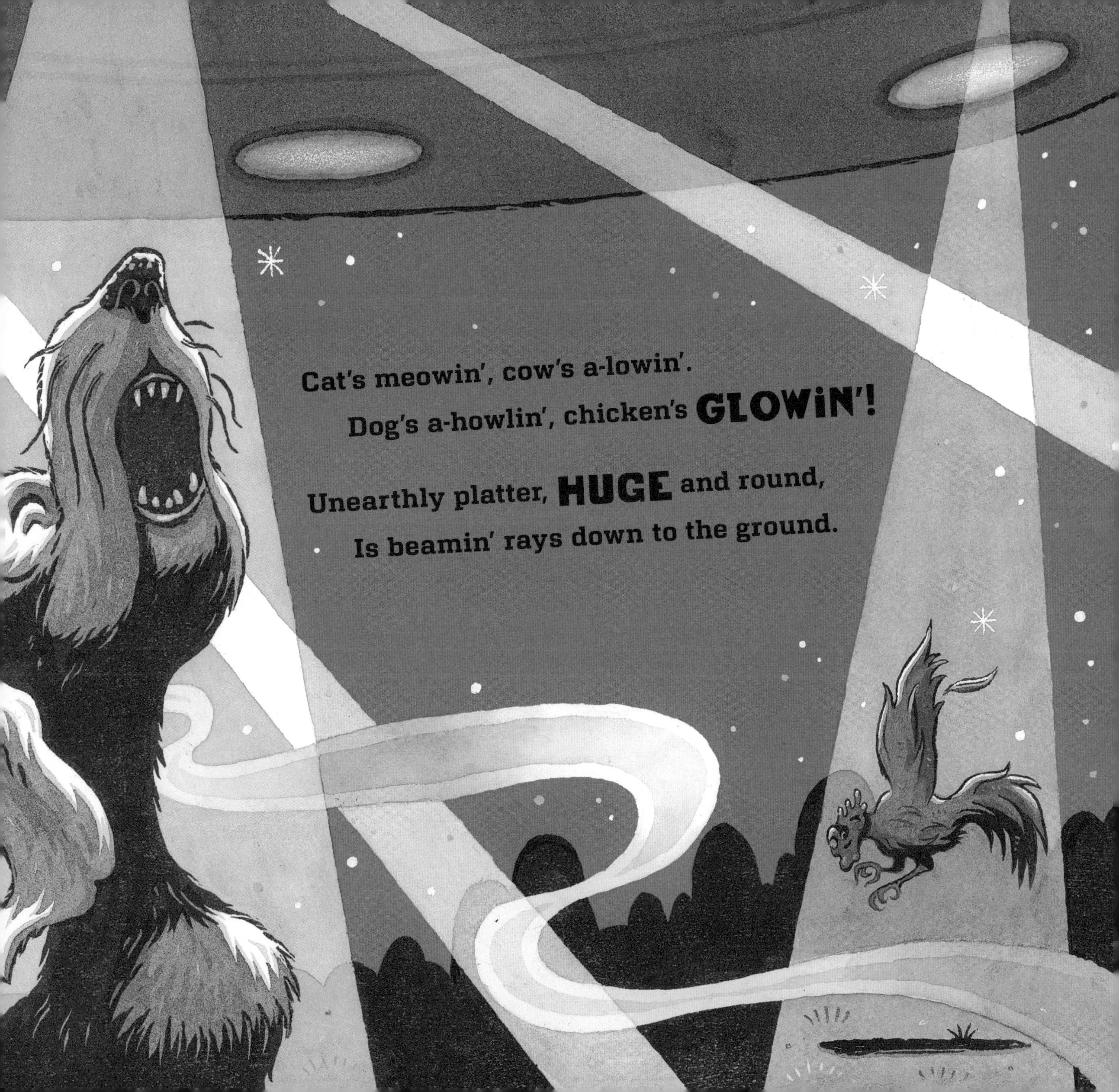

Cat's meowin', cow's a-lowin'.
Dog's a-howlin', chicken's **GLOWiN'!**

Unearthly platter, **HUGE** and round,
Is beamin' rays down to the ground.

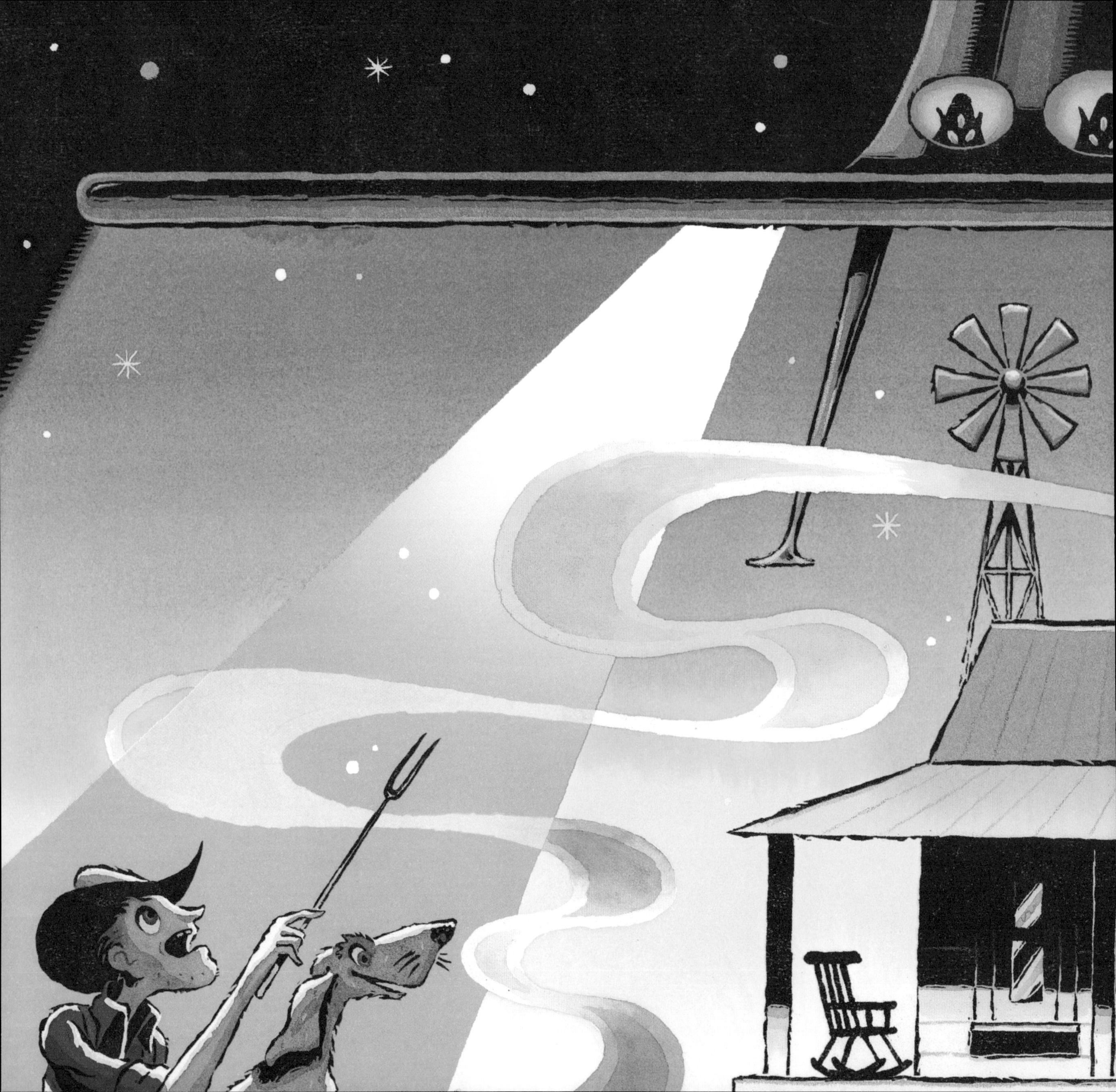

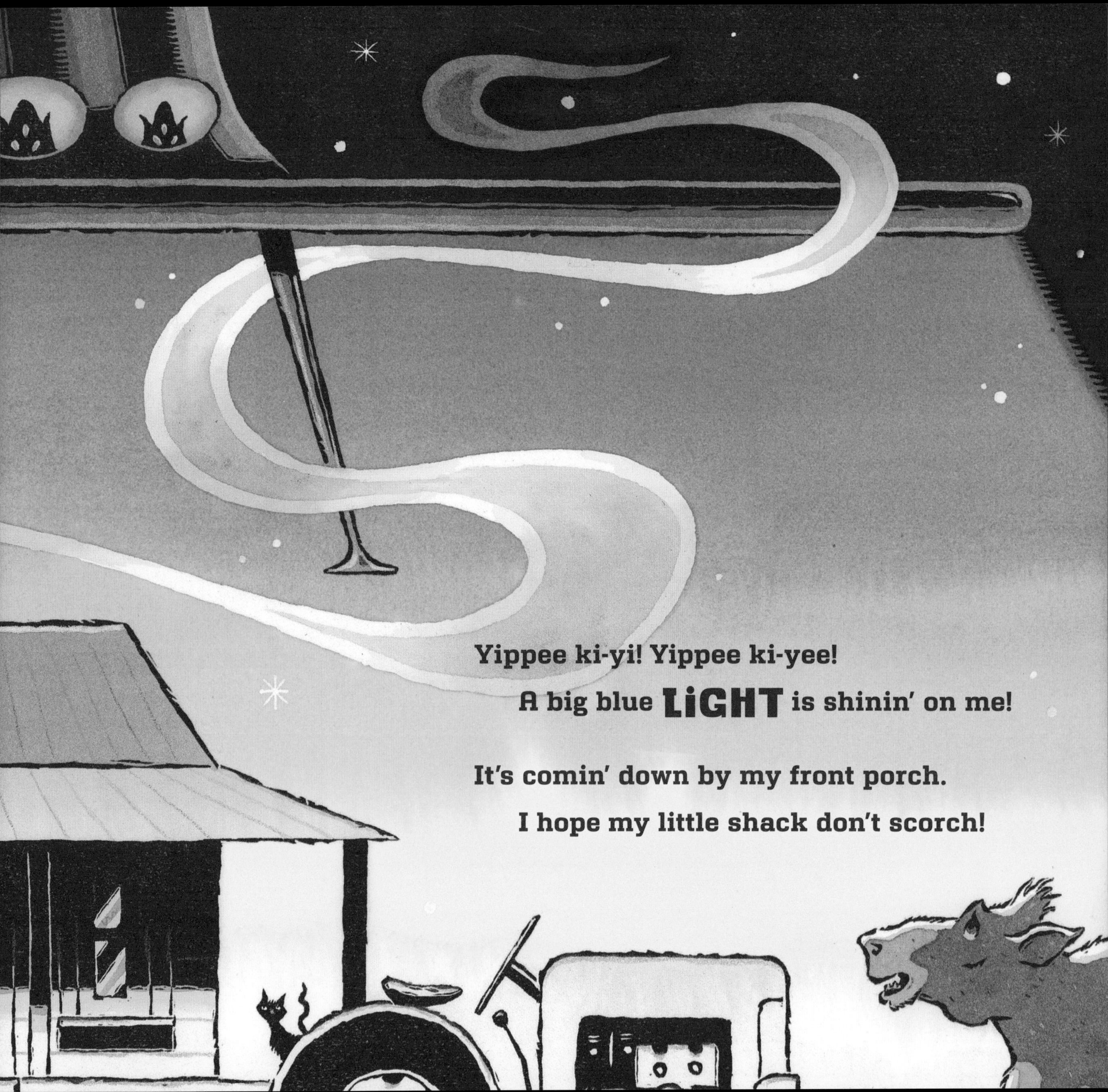

Yippee ki-yi! Yippee ki-yee!

A big blue **LIGHT** is shinin' on me!

It's comin' down by my front porch.

I hope my little shack don't scorch!

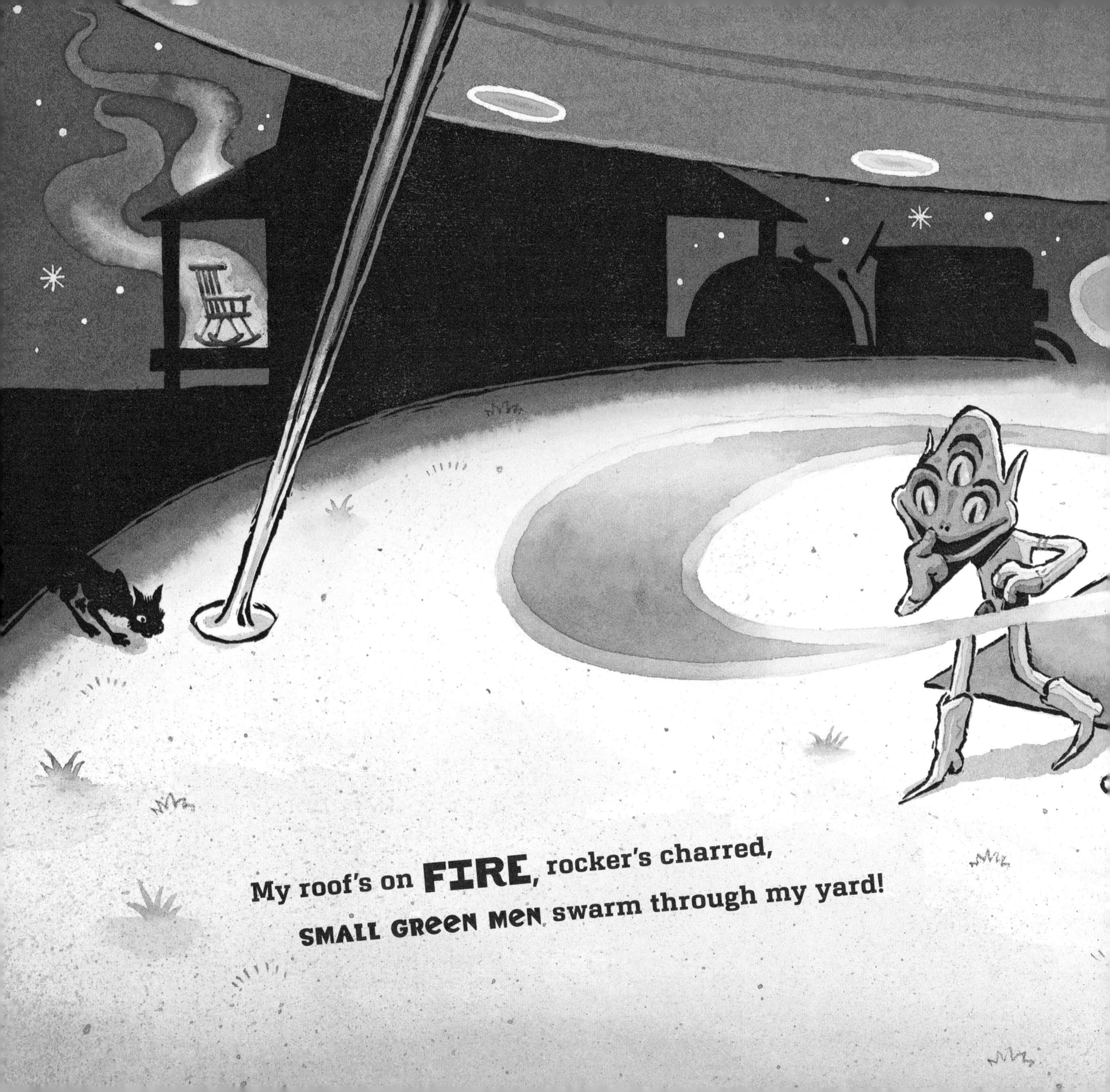

My roof's on **FIRE**, rocker's charred,

SMALL GREEN MEN swarm through my yard!

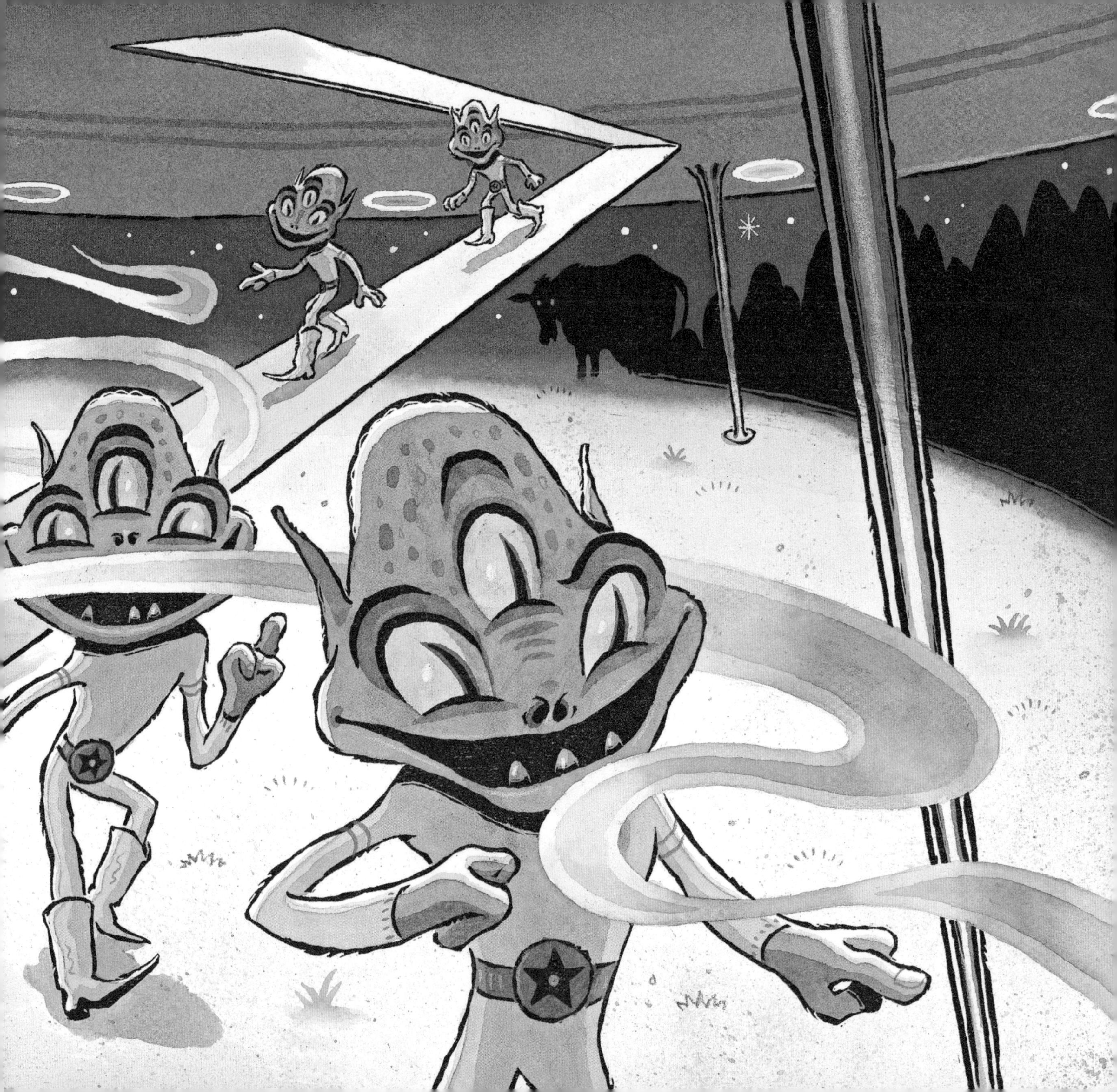

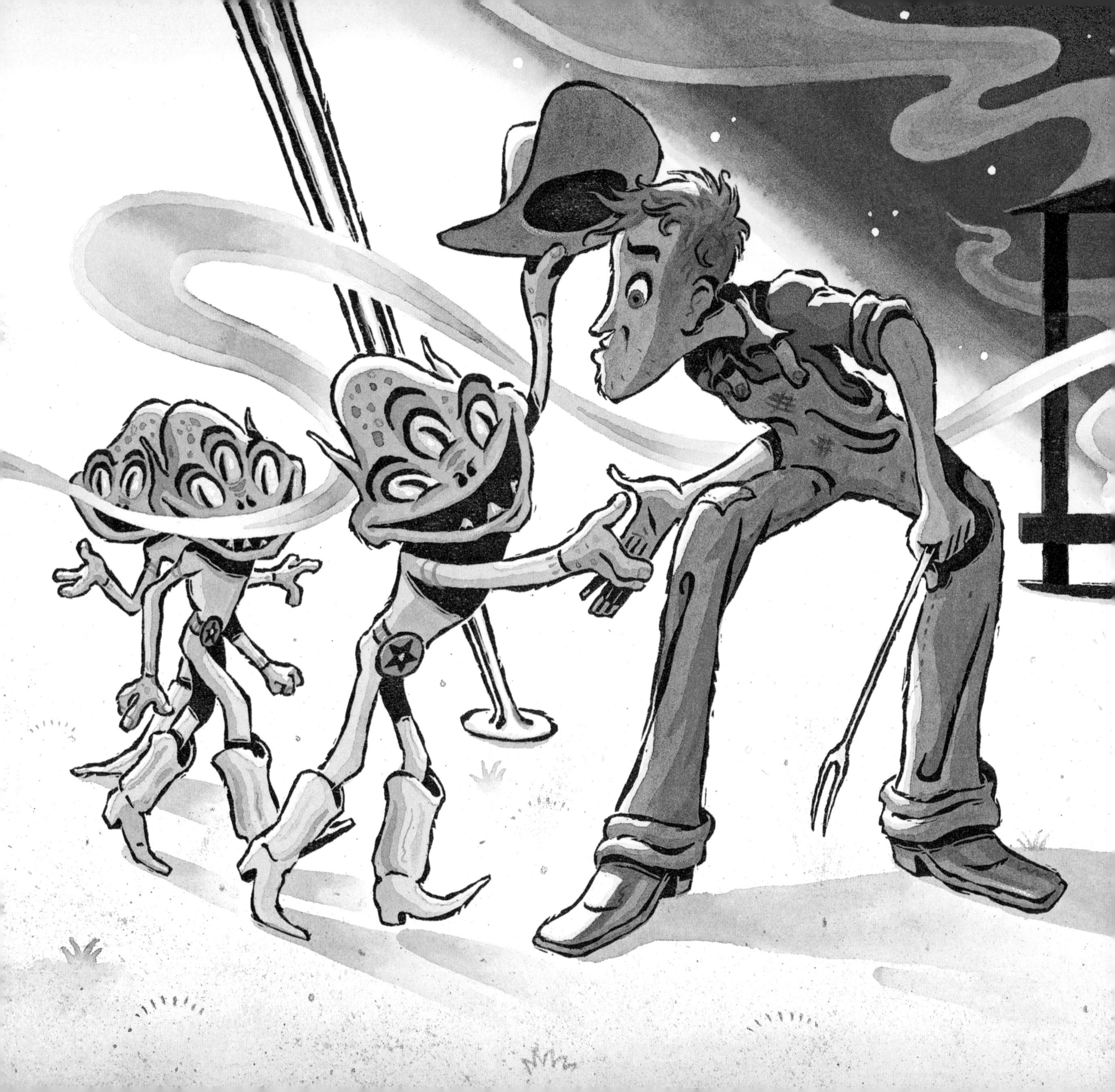

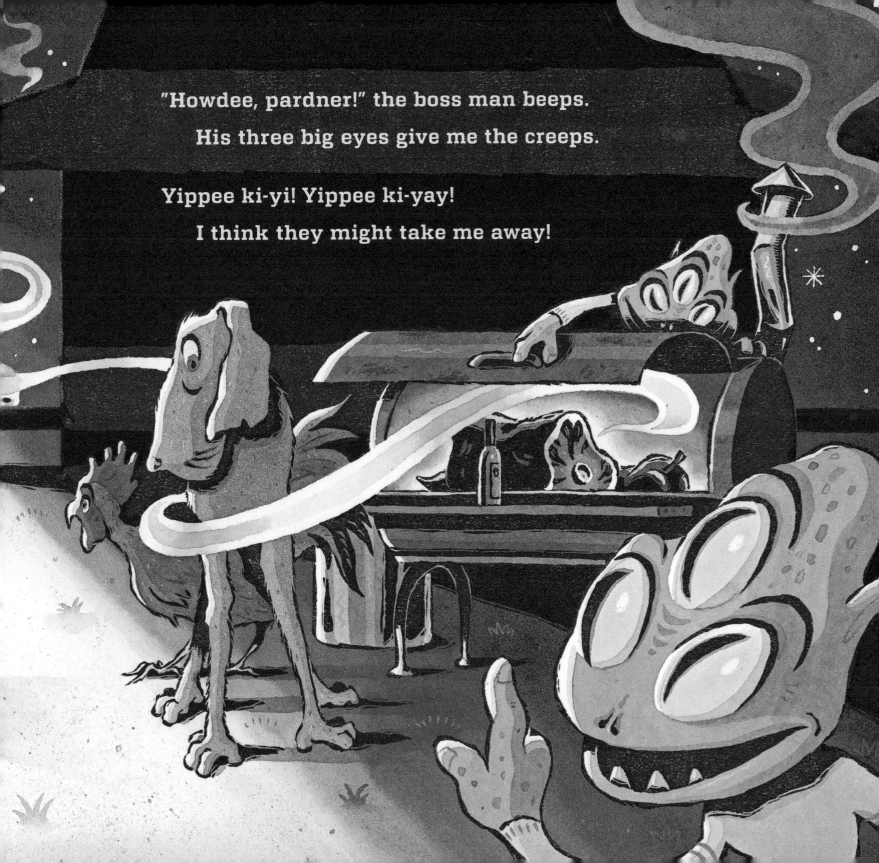

"Howdee, pardner!" the boss man beeps.

His three big eyes give me the creeps.

Yippee ki-yi! Yippee ki-yay!

I think they might take me away!

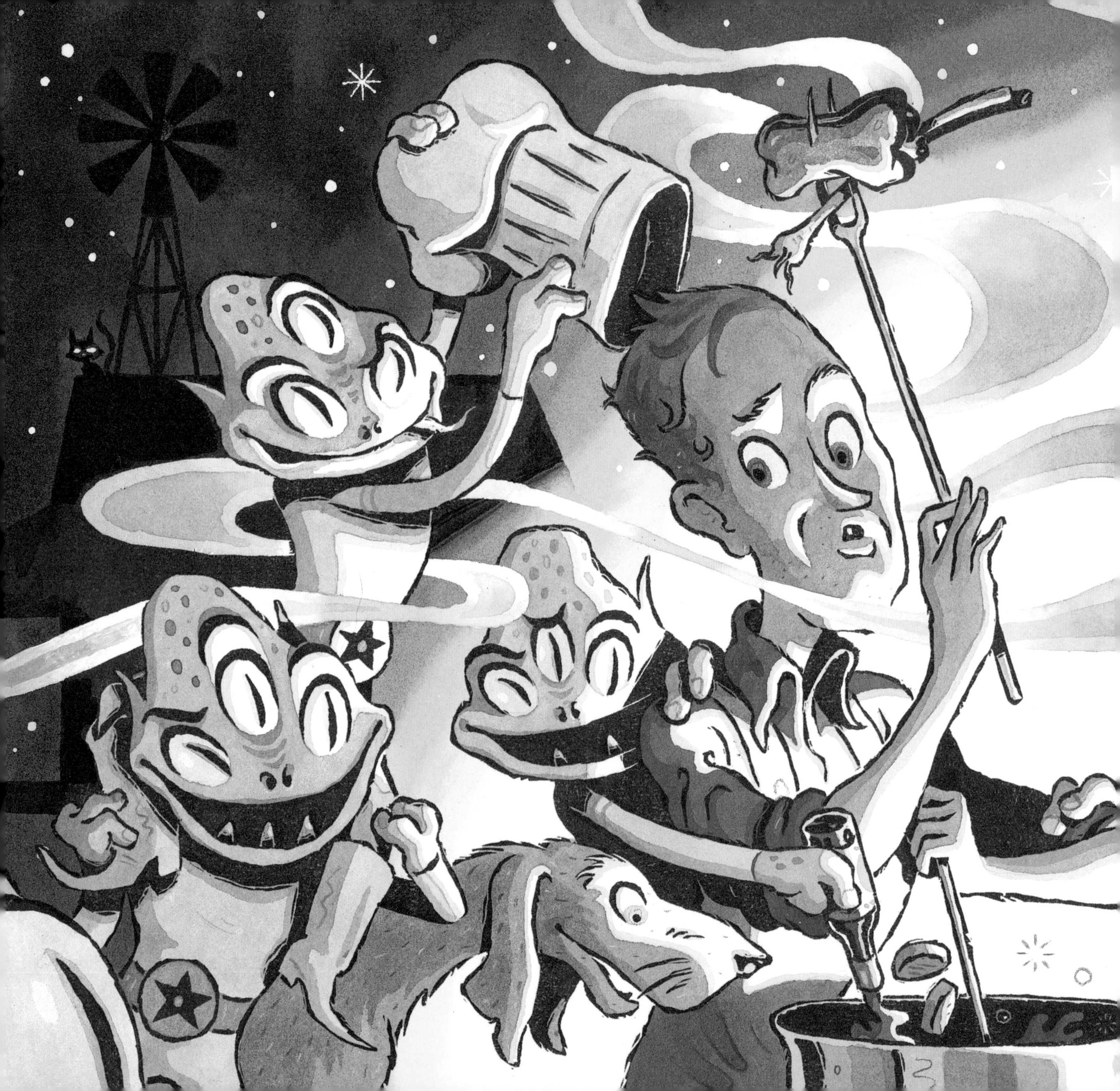

"We don't want your leader, Willy,

Just your **BARBECUE** and chili."

Fire up the grill, put on the beans.

Chop up peppers, taters, and greens.

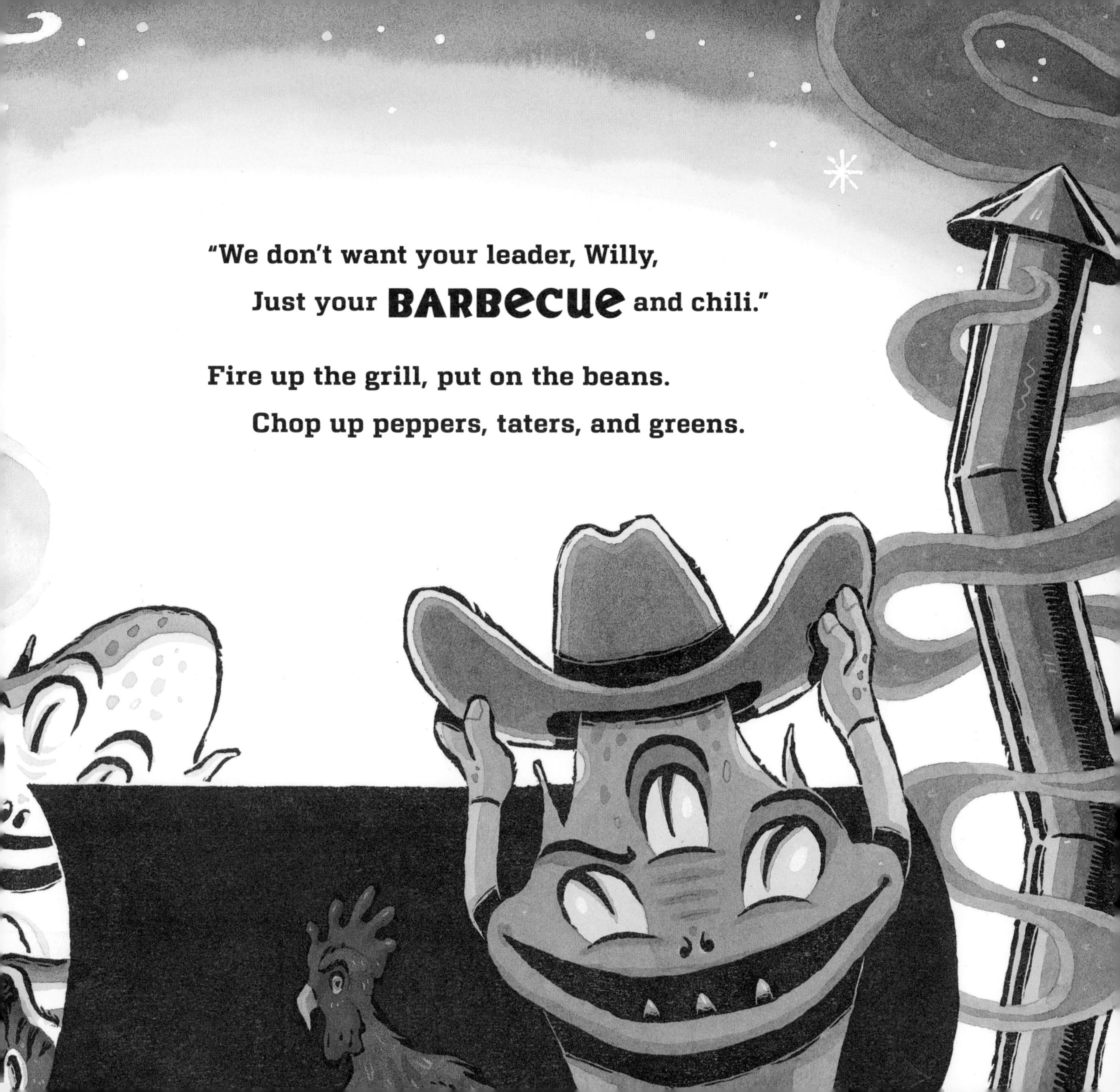

Little guys eat barbecue,

Then gobble up my **HAT** and **SHOES.**

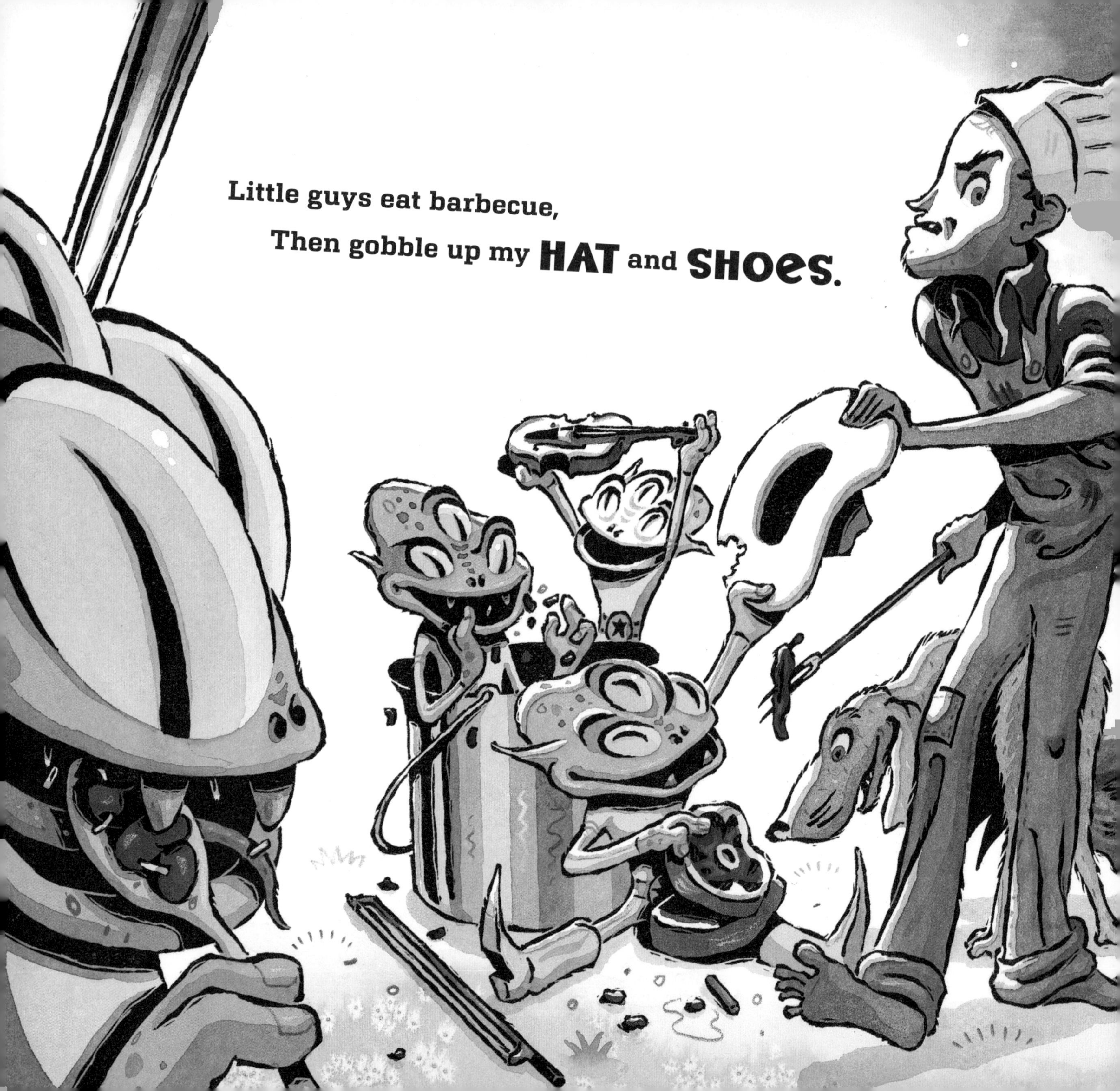

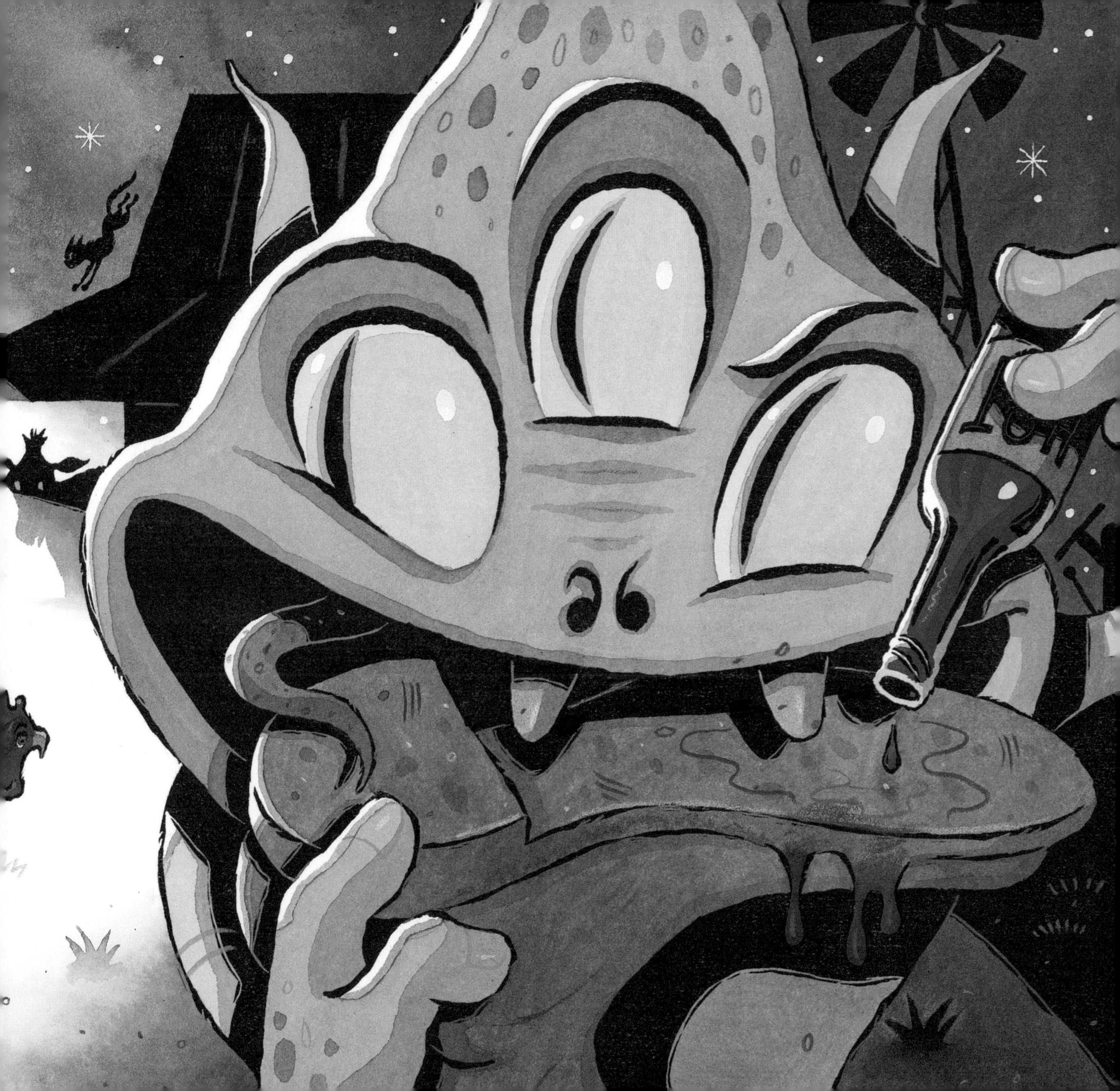

Yippee ki-yi! Yippee ki-yoo!
Green men line up two by two.

"Willy, we want to **DO-Si-DO**.
Play your fiddle a-fore we go."

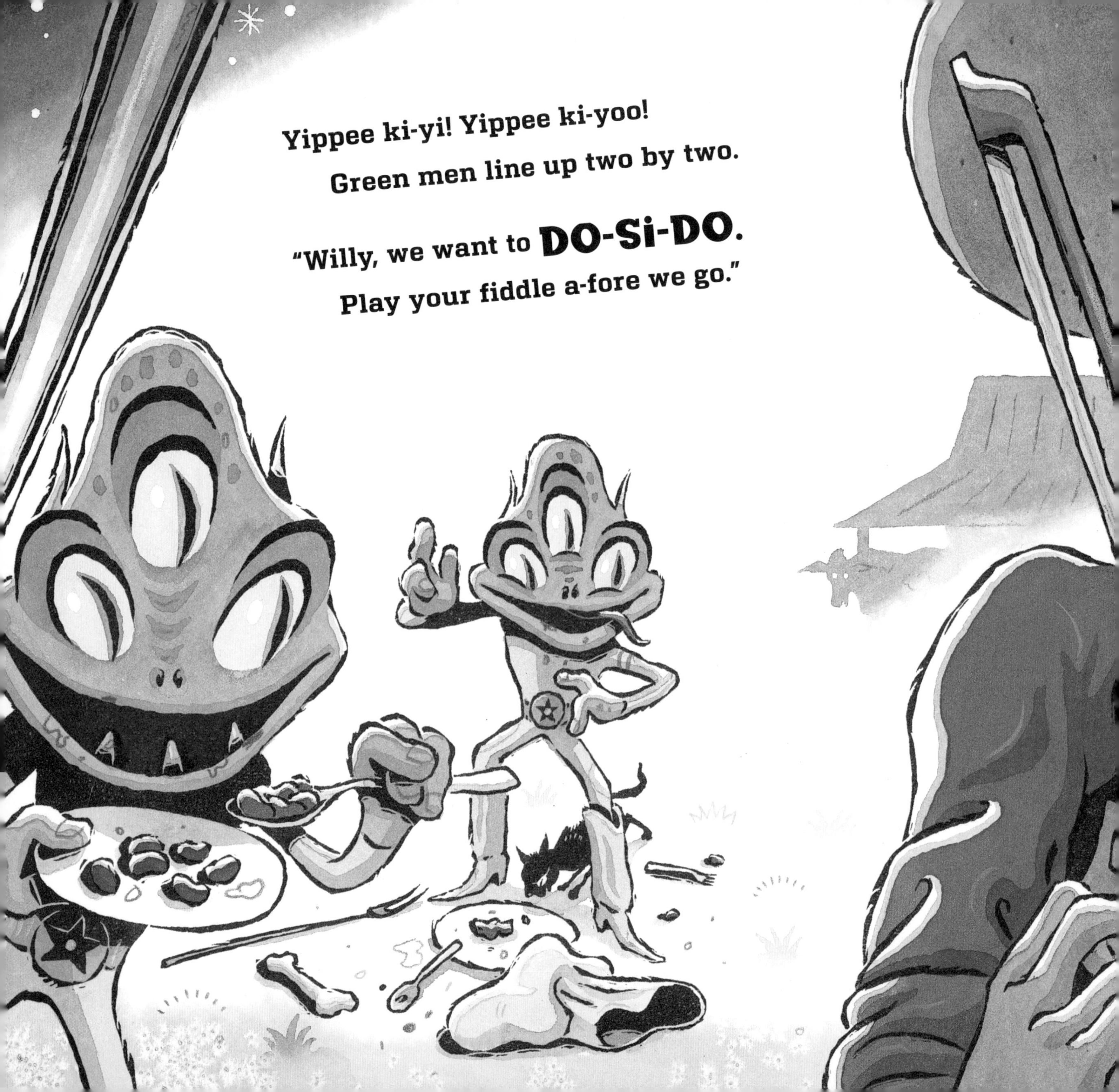

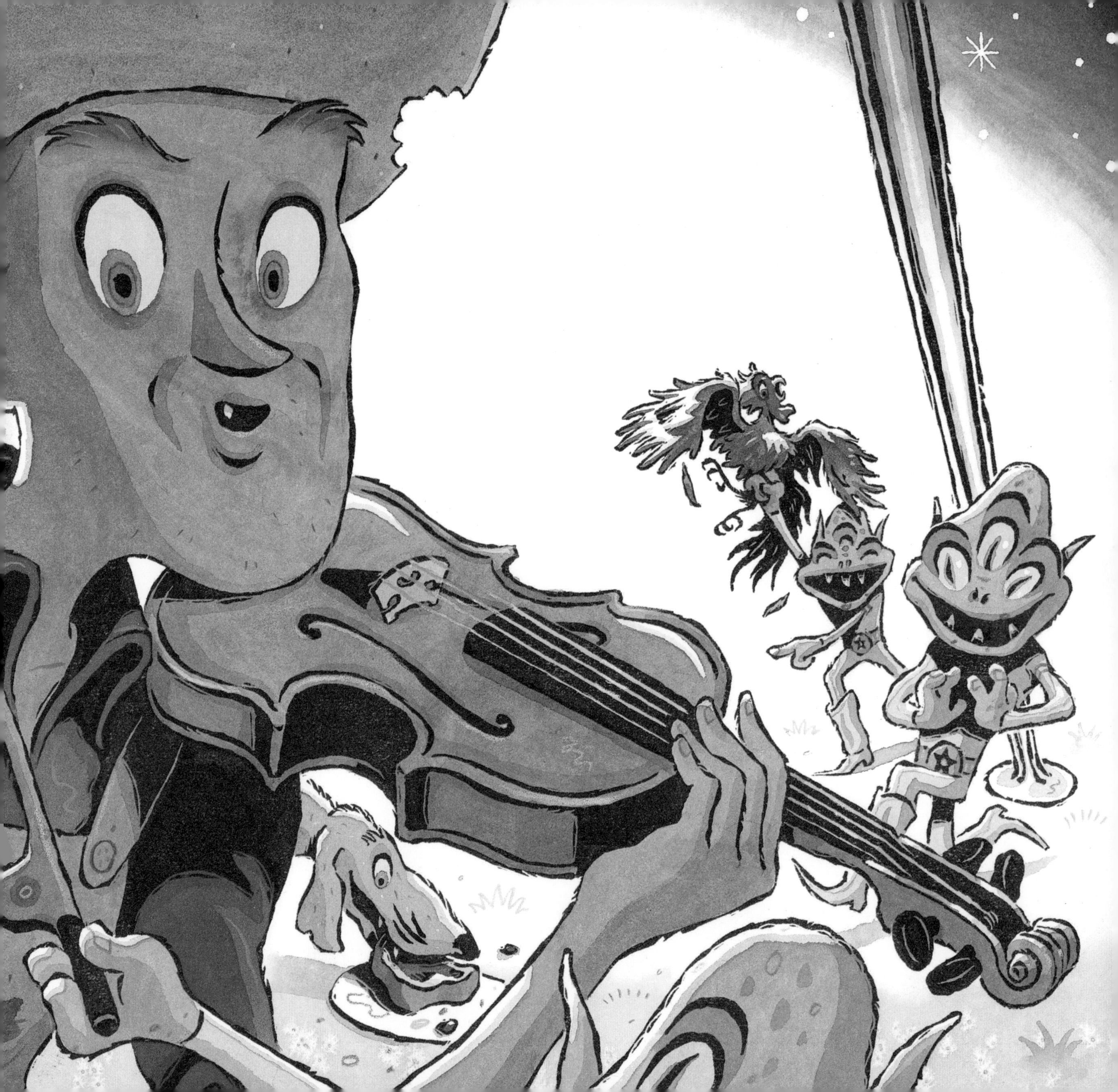

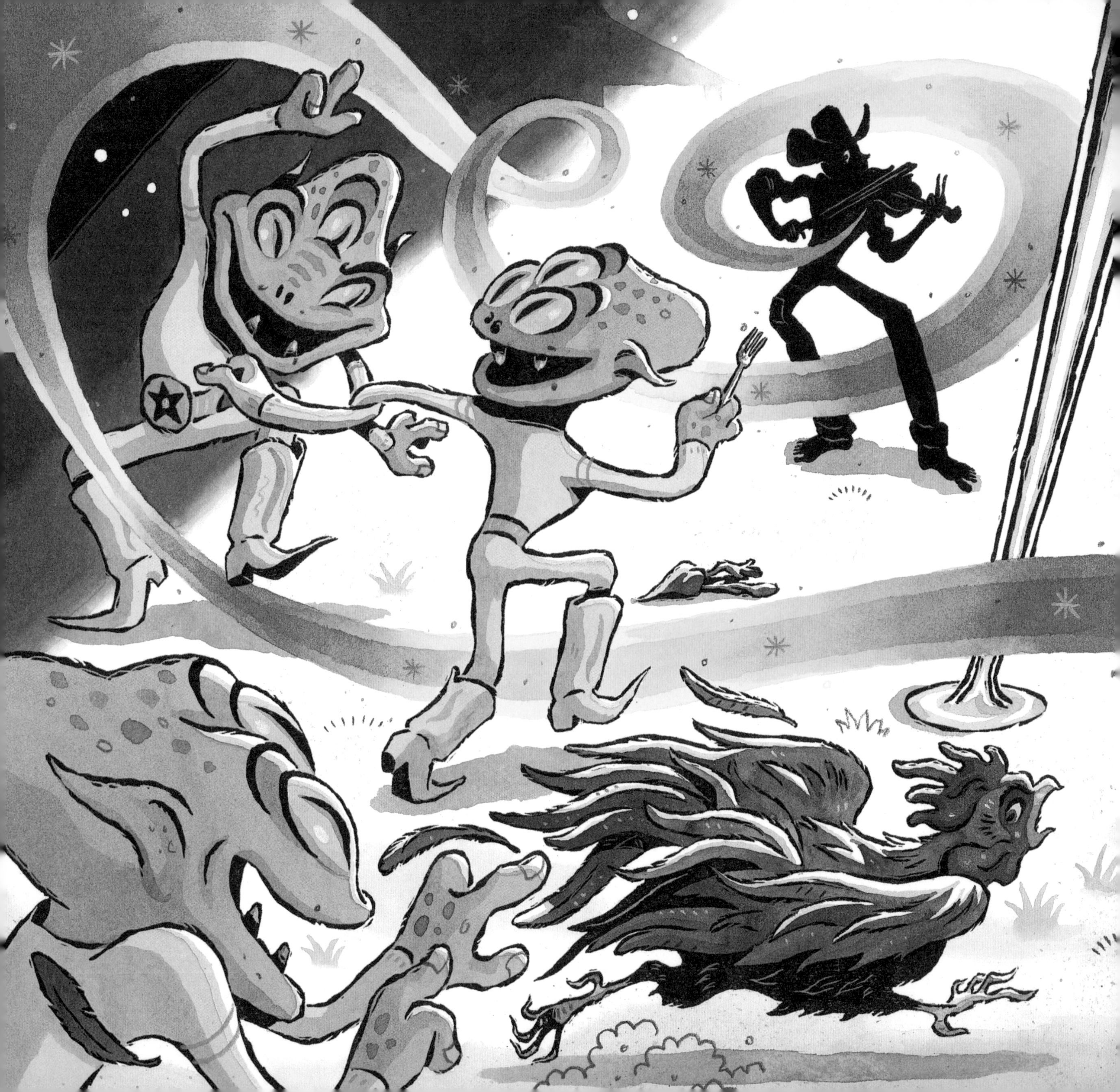

Greenies **TWO-STEP** mighty hard;
They wear a hole plumb through my yard.

Those little fellas just won't stop;
I keep on fiddlin' 'til they drop.

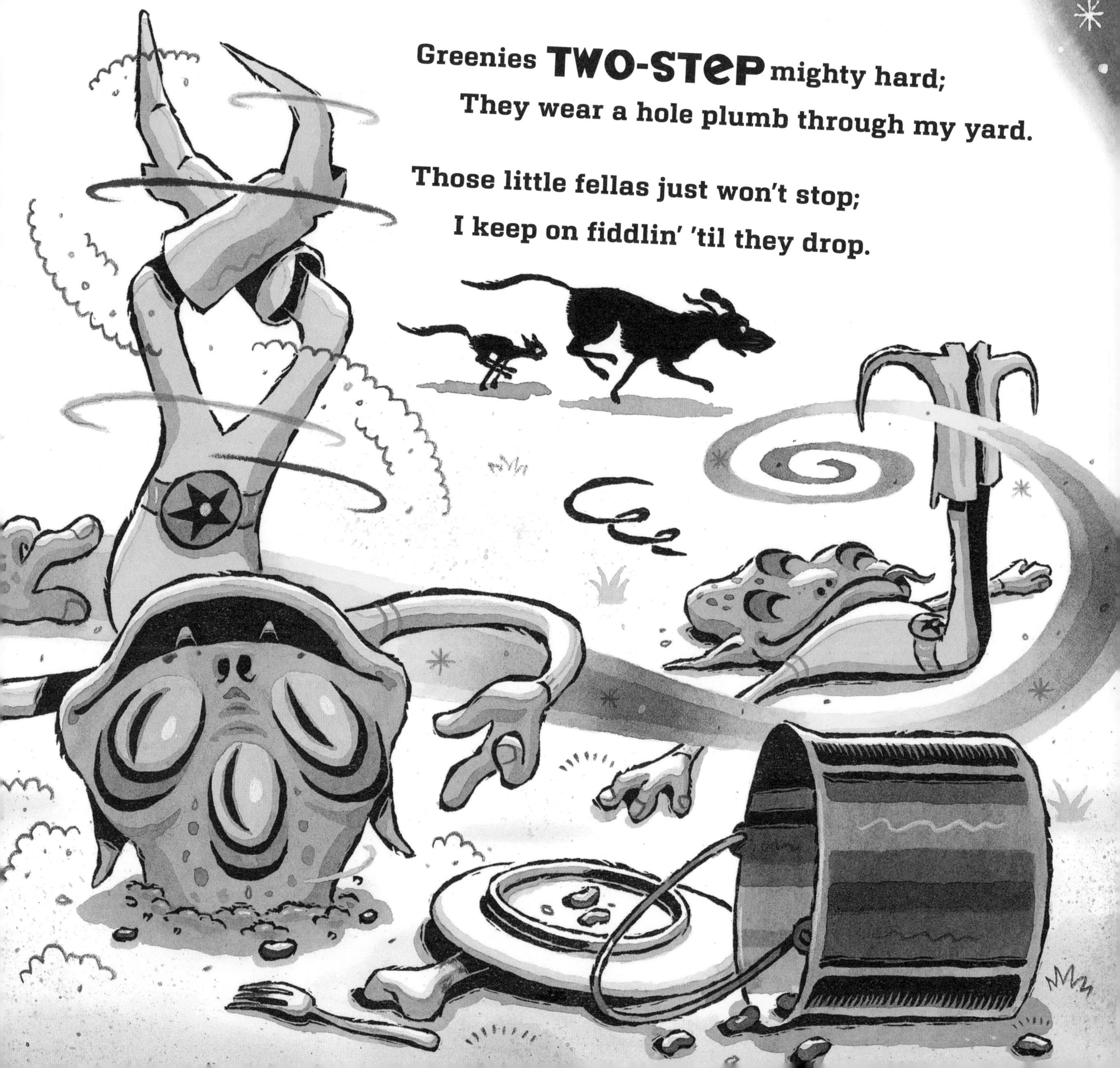

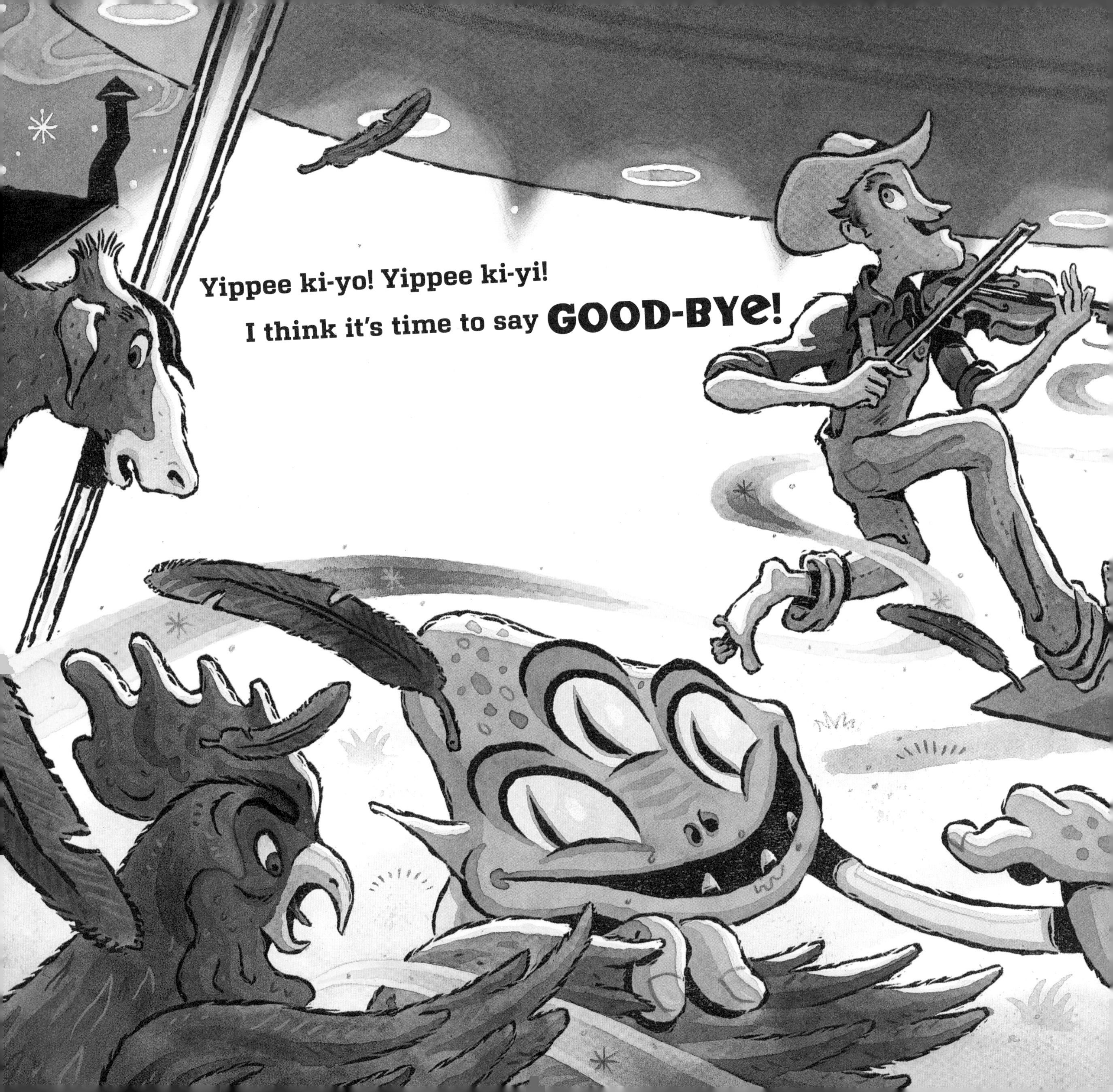

Yippee ki-yo! Yippee ki-yi!

I think it's time to say **GOOD-BYE!**

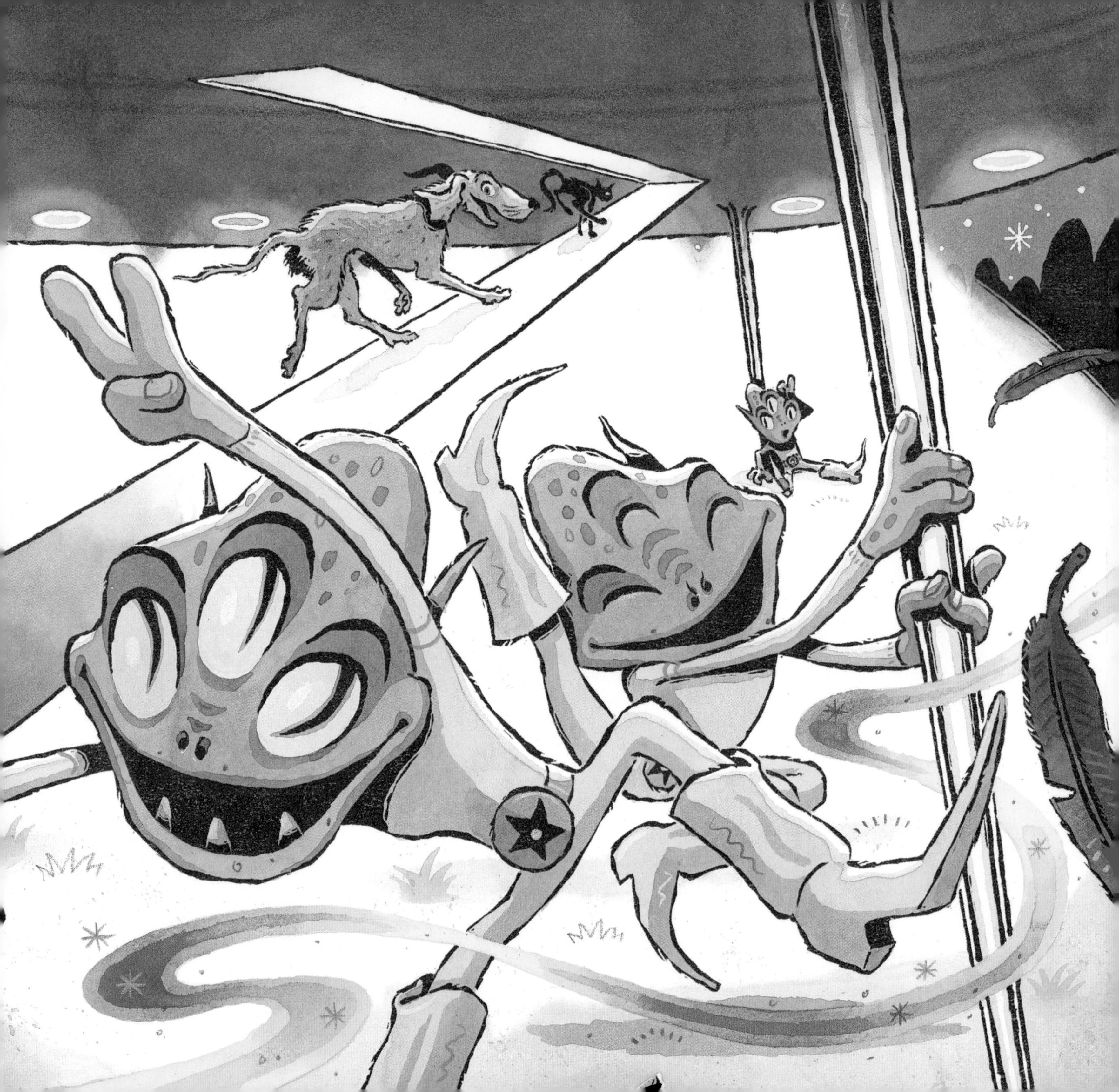

So long, GREENIES! Enjoy your stay.
I'm goin' for a HOLIDAY!

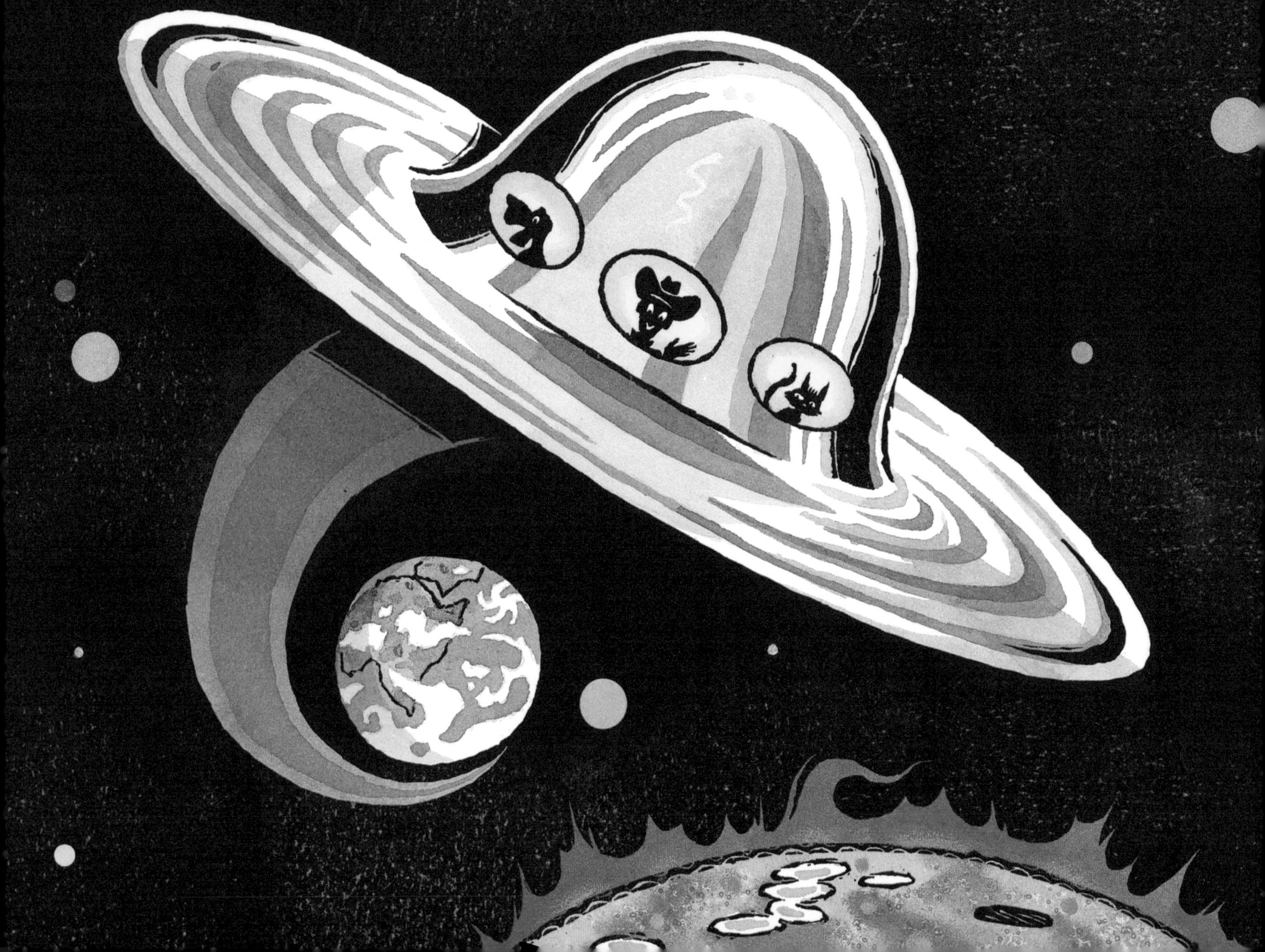

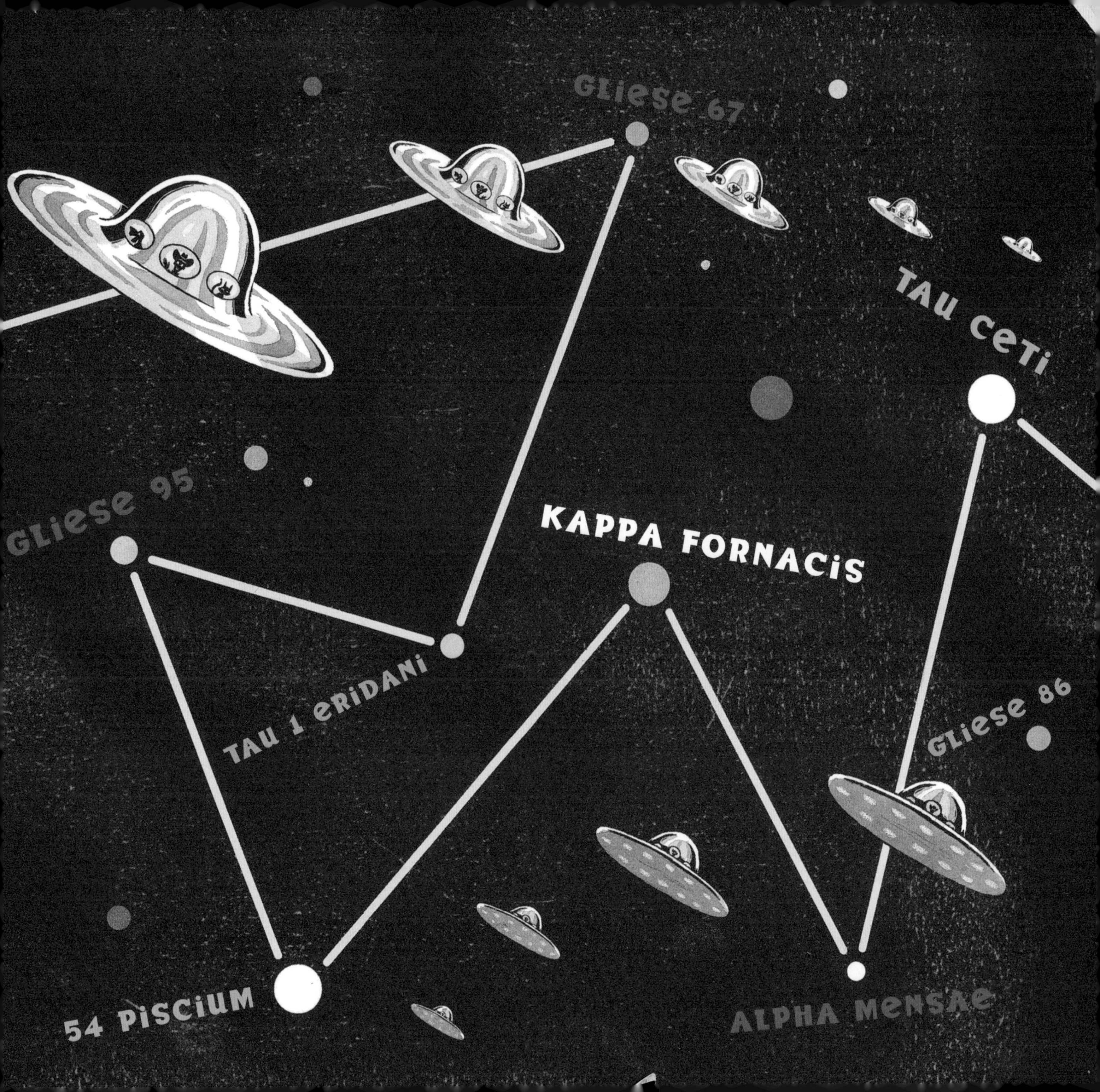

GLIESE 67
TAU CETI
GLIESE 95
KAPPA FORNACIS
TAU 1 ERIDANI
GLIESE 86
54 PISCIUM
ALPHA MENSAE

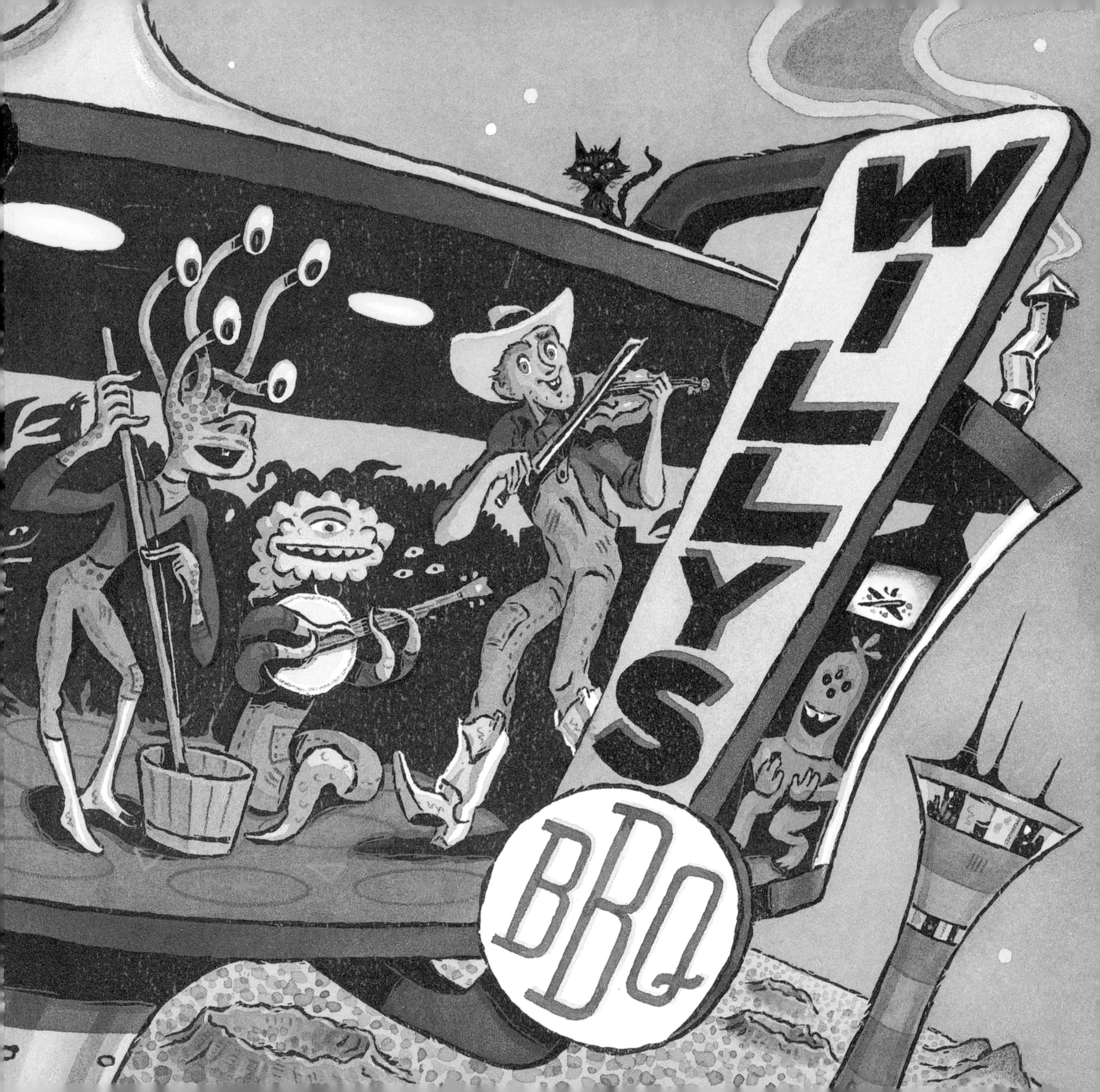
WILLY'S
BBQ

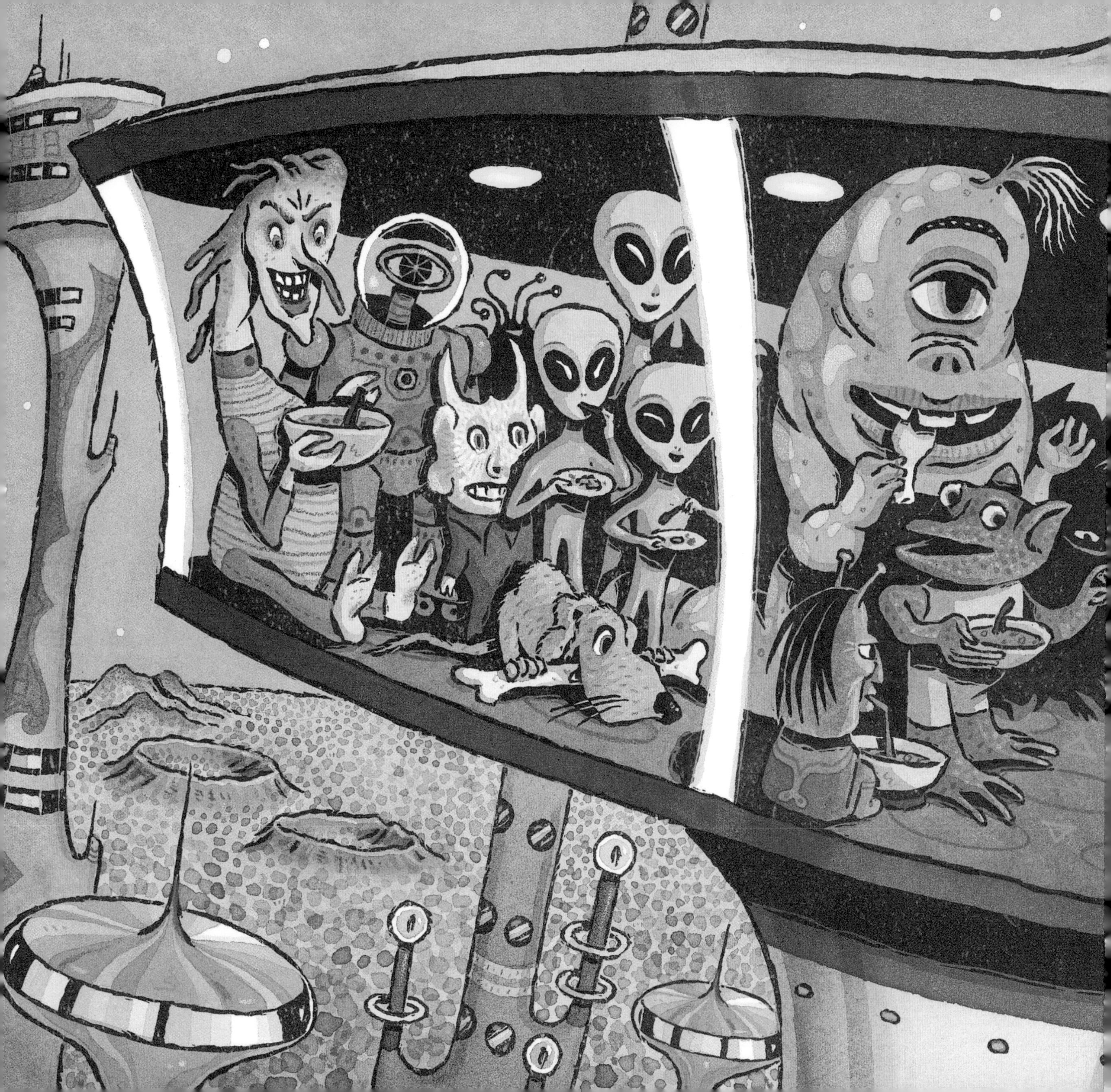

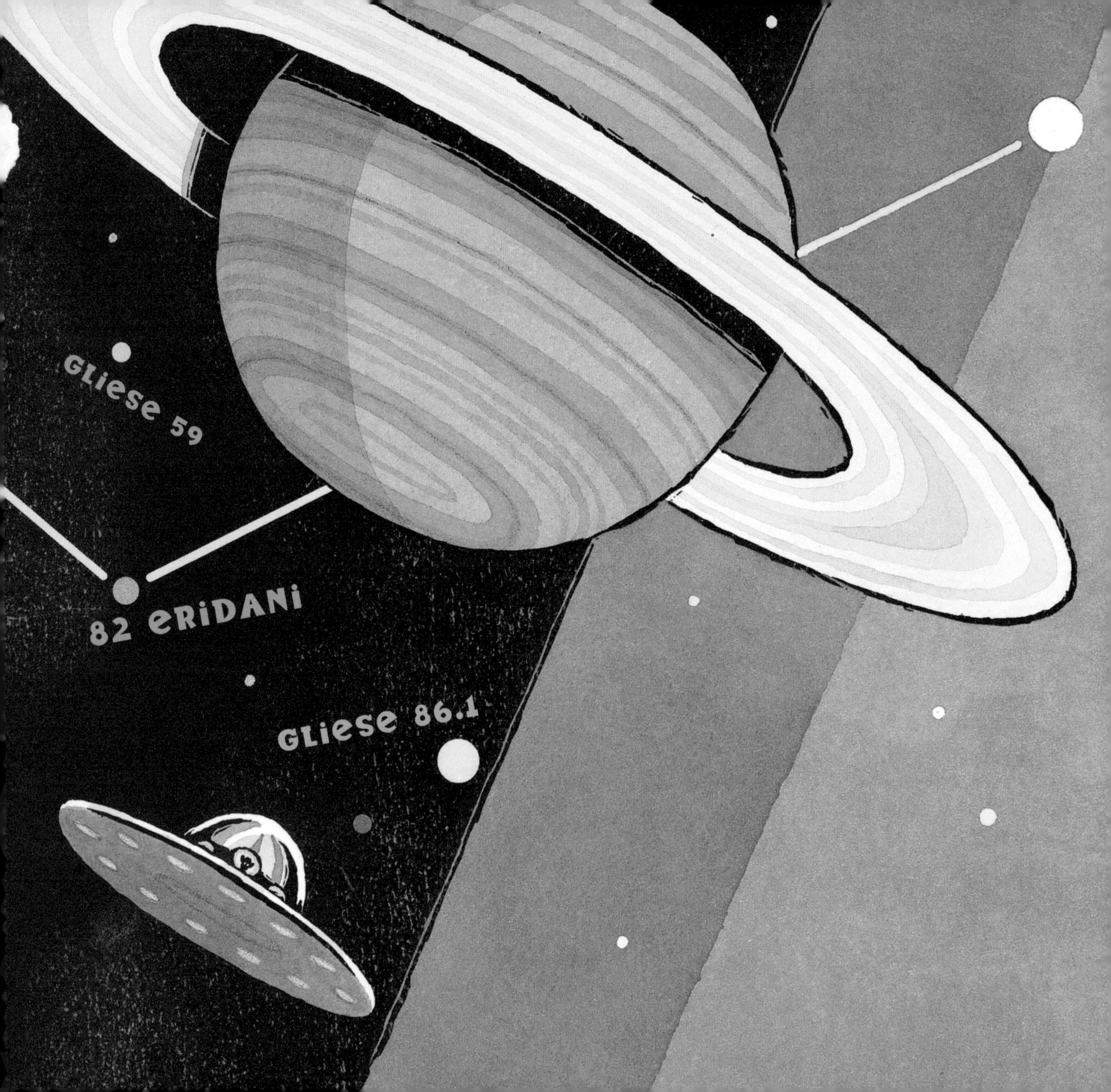
GLiese 59
82 eRiDANi
GLiese 86.1

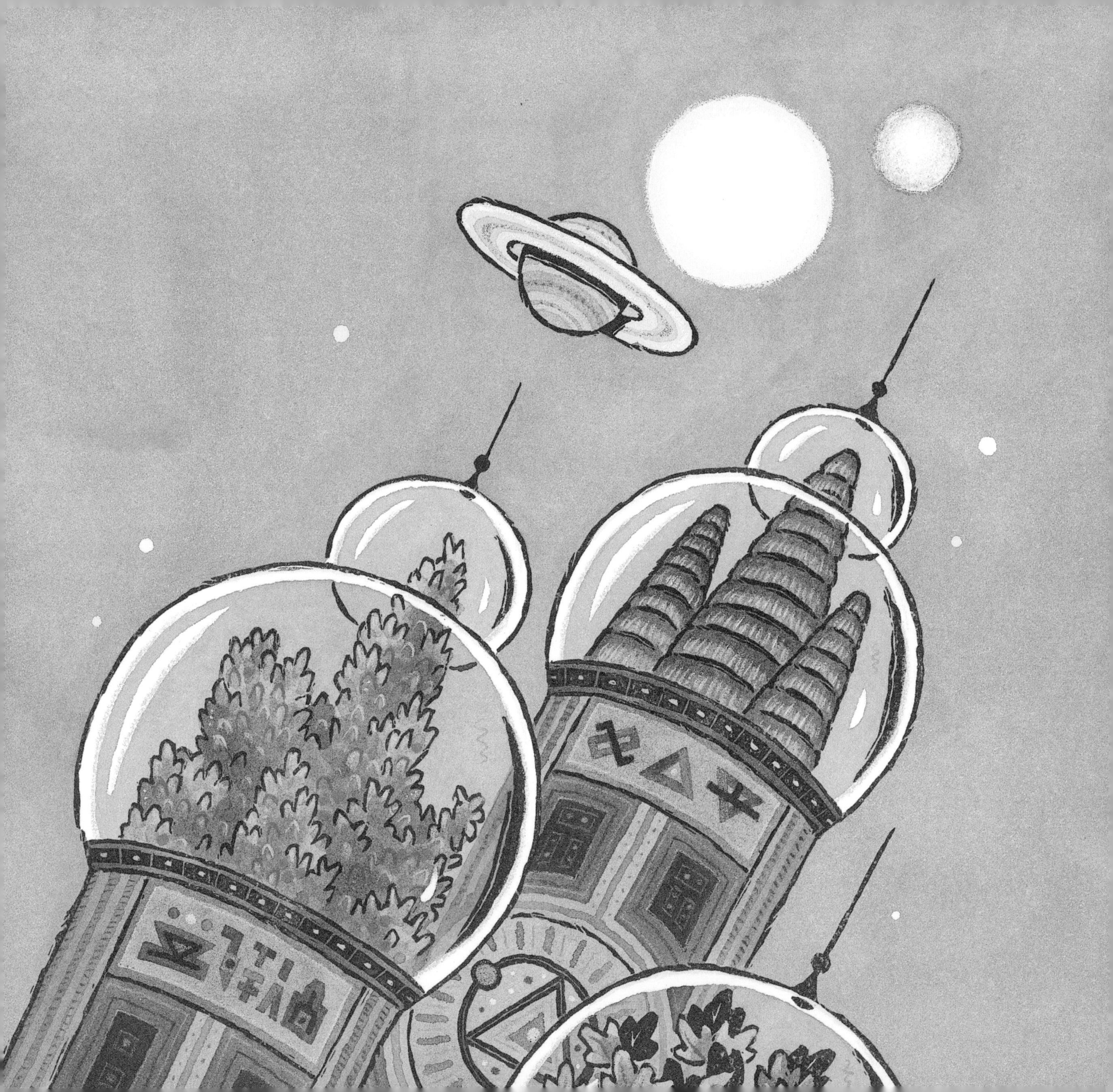

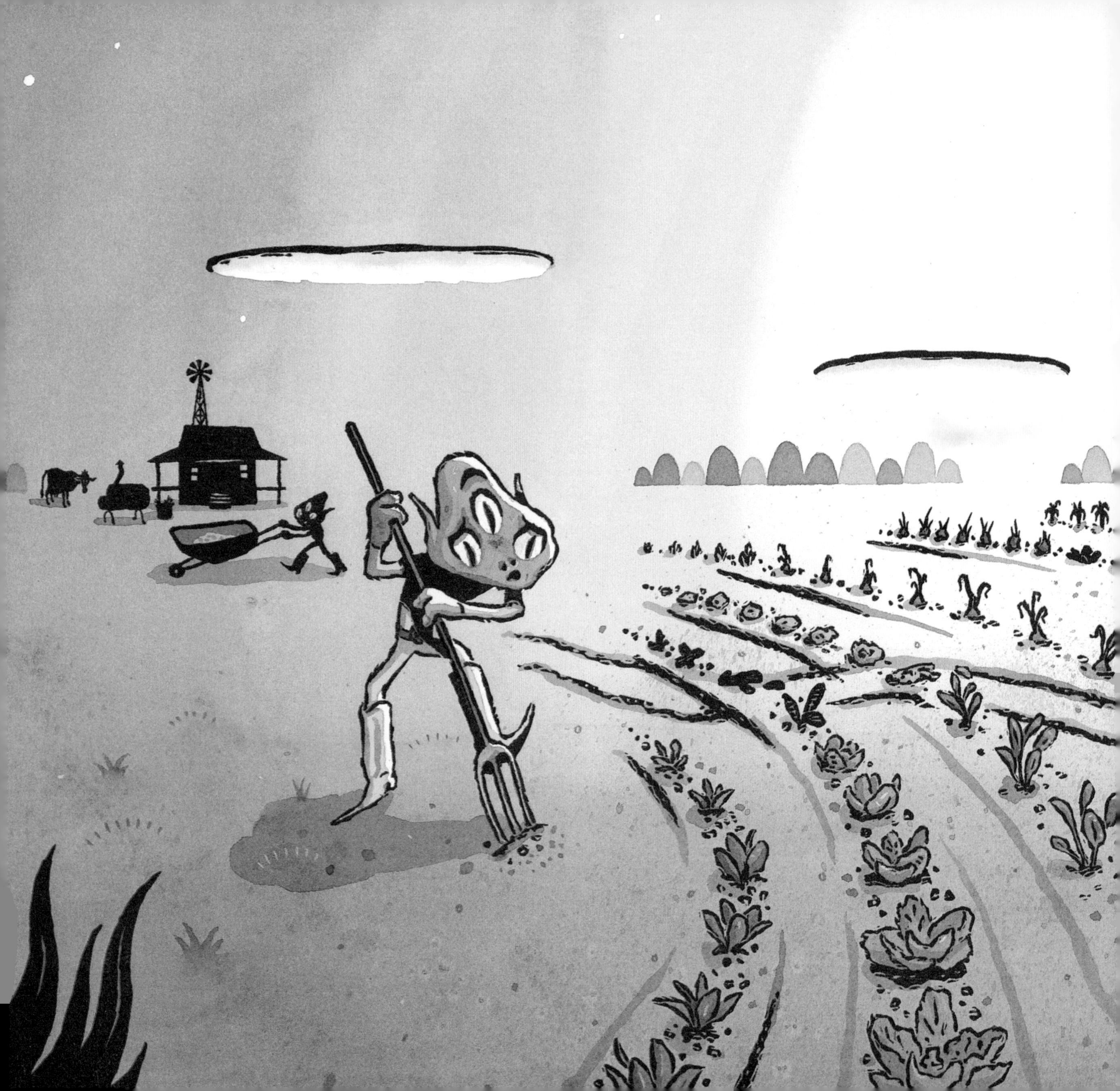

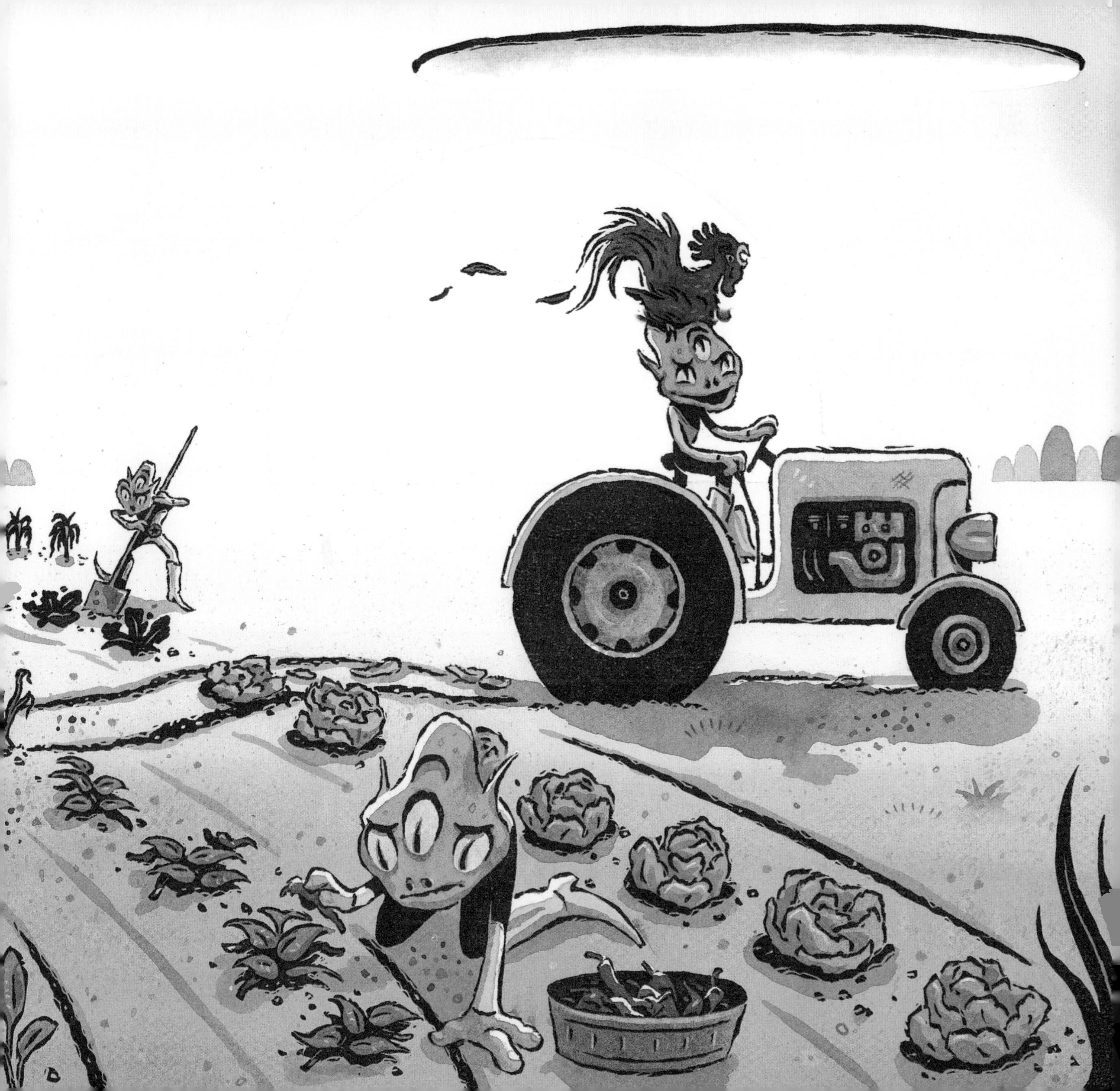

WiLLY'S OUT OF THiS WORLD BARBeCUe SAUCe

¼ cup vinegar
½ cup water
2 tablespoons sugar
1 tablespoon prepared mustard
¼ teaspoon pepper
2 teaspoons salt
¼ teaspoon cayenne pepper
Several slices of lemon
Several slices of onion
¼ cup butter
¾ cup catsup
2 tablespoons Worcestershire sauce
1½ teaspoons liquid smoke

Mix first ten ingredients in saucepan; simmer 20 minutes, uncovered. Add catsup and last two ingredients. Bring to a boil. Makes about 2 cups.

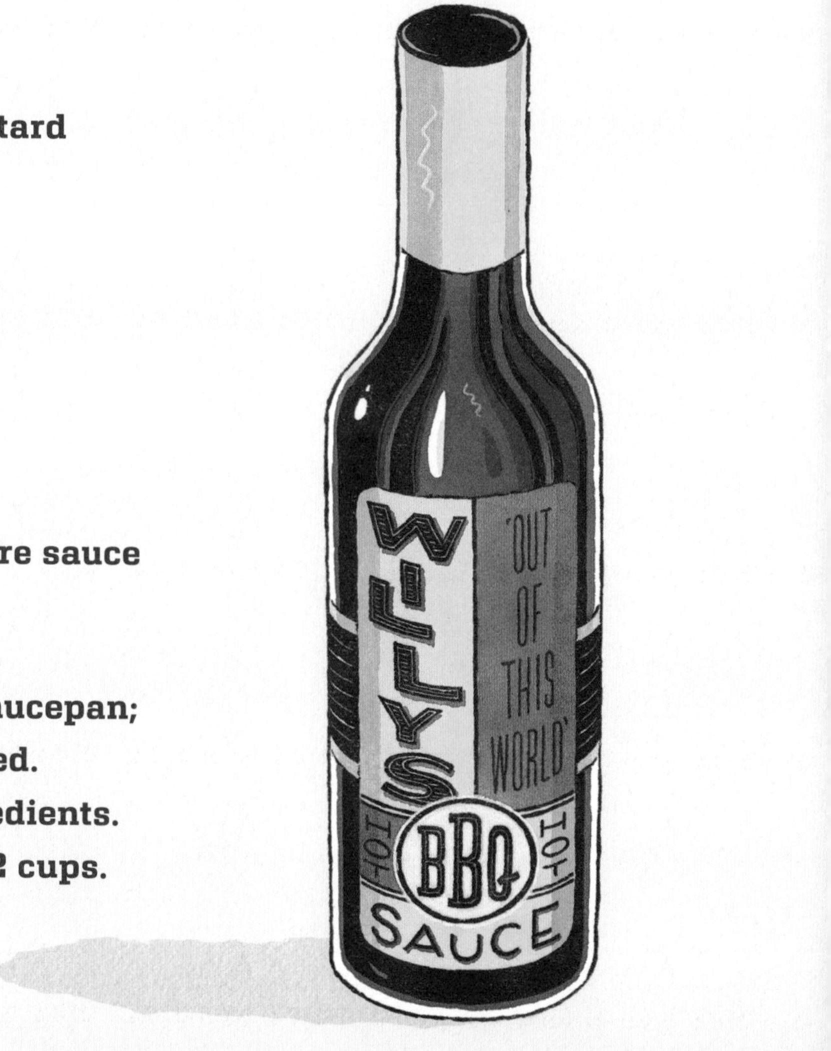
WILLYS
'OUT OF THIS WORLD'
HOT
BBQ
HOT
SAUCE

**To Jon Paul Hamilton, Jr.,
who's out of this world!** —K.D.

**For Dugald Stermer,
interstellar art cowboy** —A.M.

Text copyright © 2013 by Kathy Duval

Illustrations copyright © 2013 by Adam McCauley

Book design by Cynthia Wigginton

All rights reserved. Published by Disney • Hyperion Books, an imprint of Disney Book Group. No part of this book

may be reproduced or transmitted in any form or by any means, electronic or mechanical, including photocopying,

recording, or by any information storage and retrieval system, without written permission from the publisher.

For information address Disney • Hyperion Books, 114 Fifth Avenue, New York, New York 10011-5690.

First Edition

10 9 8 7 6 5 4 3 2 1

F383-2370-2-12335

Printed in China

Library of Congress Cataloging-in-Publication Data

Duval, Kathy.

Take me to your BBQ / Kathy Duval ; illustrated by Adam McCauley.

p. cm.

Summary: When Willy goes outside to check on his grill, he finds a UFO full of aliens who want some of his barbecue

and chili, and then tear up his farm square dancing while he plays the fiddle. Includes a recipe for barbecue sauce.

ISBN 978-1-4231-2255-5

[1. Stories in rhyme. 2. Extraterrestrial beings—Fiction. 3. Barbecuing—Fiction. 4. Square dancing—Fiction.

5. Humorous stories.] I. McCauley, Adam, ill. II. Title. III. Title: Take me to your barbecue.

PZ8.3.D946Tak 2013

[E]—dc23   2012016101

Reinforced binding

Visit www.disneyhyperionbooks.com

Publisher's Note:

The recipe contained in this book is to be followed exactly as written, under adult supervision. The Publisher

is not responsible for your specific health or allergy needs that may require medical supervision.

The Publisher is not responsible for any adverse reactions to the recipe contained in this book.

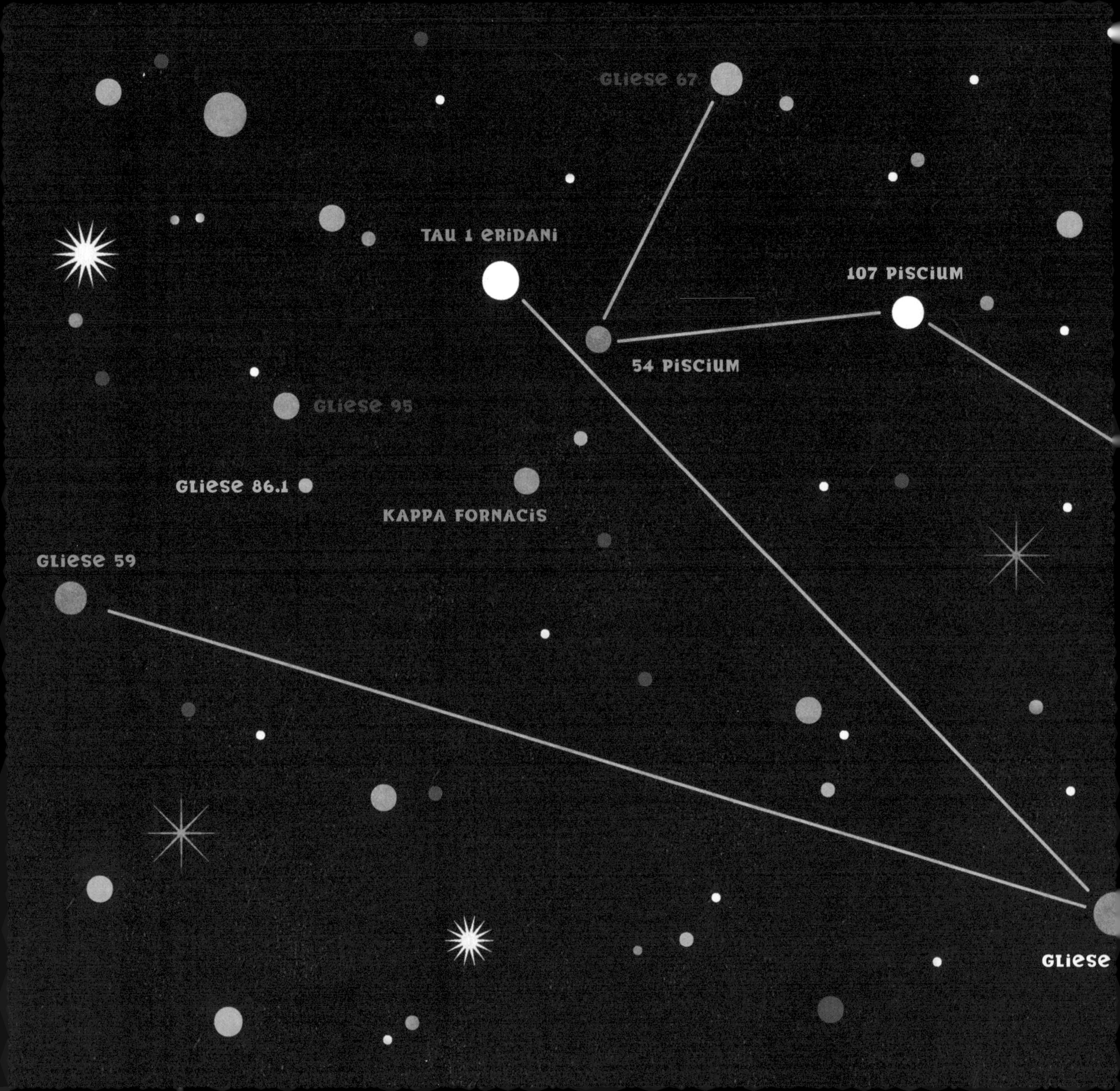
GLIESE 67
TAU 1 ERIDANI
107 PISCIUM
54 PISCIUM
GLIESE 95
GLIESE 86.1
KAPPA FORNACIS
GLIESE 59
GLIESE